I0571586

Treasure of Mine

A Precious Reuben Novel.

Published in the United States of America by Old Game Press.

http://www.precious-fictions.com

Dedication

This novel is dedicated to those who keep an open heart so that love can find its way in.

Acknowledgment

Special thanks go to God almighty that made everything possible by sending loyal and encouraging friends and family my way to make this novel a success.

"Without support and encouragement, dreams are nothing more than thoughts hidden in the mind of the dreamer." – Precious Reuben.

Chapter 1

Chief Ndube and Martha his wife stood patiently at the airport staring into the crowded arrival hall. They were waiting for their daughter Stella who had traveled to Canada seven years earlier and was returning that day. Chief Ndube kept pointing at black men leaving the airport with their Caucasian wives. He turned to his wife while still watching out for Stella and said, "Look at that, look at what our young men have turned into. They have abandoned the well-mannered girls in our land to marry *oyibo* – Caucasian women!" Martha pretended not to hear what her husband said. She stretched her neck further, peering into the crowd as if it would enable her see their daughter quicker. Chief Ndube continued as he focused on another young couple leaving the airport. "Look at that one; is she better looking than our girls?"

Martha despised the way her husband reacted to interracial marriages. She wondered, if it weren't for his wealth, whether he would speak that way and consider his opinions so full of veracity. She drew a long breath and turned to him saying, "*Nkem* – my love, the world is fast changing, so whatever reason that makes a man decide to marry a woman outside his culture is totally up to him." But Chief Ndube wasn't satisfied with his wife's reply. He needed to help her understand. "Are you saying that those *oyibo* can pound yams and cook *egusi* soup?" he asked playfully.

"Pounded yam and *egusi* soup is not the only

reason why people get married. I believe that those people fell in love and decided to get married. If the woman can't prepare it then the man can teach her." She replied calmly.

"And what if he doesn't know how to cook?" he interrupted, impishly. "Then they both can learn. By the way, don't tell me the only reason why you married me is because of *egusi* soup and pounded yam?" Chief Ndube laughed out loud, drawing attention to himself. He placed his right arm on her shoulder and whispered, "You and I both know that's not true." Martha smiled and gave him a weak look. "Oh there she comes!" Chief Ndube exclaimed and pulled the wide sleeve of his *agbada* towards his shoulder and repeated the same for the left sleeve. Martha rushed to meet her daughter who was standing in the large hall with Nick, her Caucasian boyfriend.

Chief Ndube walked up to Stella, hugged her, held her both cheeks and smiled at her. He hadn't seen her in many years and hadn't been that excited since Chike, his son, had won the Young Mathematician Award. He pretended not to notice the young man standing beside her daughter. "Daddy, Mummy, I'd like you to meet Nick, my boyfriend," Stella said happily as she searched her parents' face for approval. "You are welcome here, my son," Martha said, quickly offering her hand for a shake. Nick happily shook her hand and went to hug her. Chief Ndube tried hard to contain his resentment. Without saying a word, he swatted his *agbada* once again and led them out of the airport.

They walked to the airport garage where their driver,

Mathew, was waiting at the driver's side of the jeep. Immediately, when he saw Stella pushing the heavy cart towards the car, he dashed out to greet her. He bowed quickly with a smile and began loading the boot of the Nissan Pathfinder with her luggage. Chief Ndube sat in the back of the car with his wife and stared up at Stella who was whispering to her boyfriend. He barked, "Stella! Won't you get in the car?" Stella recovered from the shout and replied calmly, knowing fully how impatient her father was, "Dad, there's no space for Nick and I. I'm thinking of calling a cab."

"What do you mean "call a cab?" Didn't you notice that we came here to take you home? Will you get in the car right now before I drag you in?" He roared this time.

"Dad," Stella continued in her calm fashion, "are you suggesting that I abandon him here at the airport? It's best we take the cab. We'll meet you at home." Stella replied firmly.

"Darling, it's okay," Martha explained to her husband. "We should be nice to our guest. It's unfortunate there's not enough room for the young man but since they want to take a cab, that's fine." Martha gestured to Mathew, and with that, Mathew drove off the airport parking lot leaving Stella and her boyfriend behind.

"Wow, that was quit an introduction to your father. Is he always like this?" Nick asked.

"No. I think he's just in a bad mood. Don't worry, he will come around," she replied, kissing him. A cab pulled in front of them. The young lovers got in, and the cab drove them home.

As the cab entered the spacious compound with small trees by the two corners, Paulina, the Chief maid ran out with a big smile on her face. She was in her fifties with a large body to match her round face and thick legs. She rubbed her wet hands on her discolored apron and waited for the cab to park properly. Then she quickly ran to the passenger side where Stella and Nick sat. She waited for them to get out of the car.

Stella blushed when she saw the woman's excitement for her arrival. She threw herself into the woman's waiting arms and squeezed her tightly, smiling. Paulina took two steps backwards to observe her properly since she was no longer the little girl she used to baby-sit. She was now a grown woman. "*Ada m, I lo nnu*--welcome, my daughter." Paulina said as she patted Stella's hand and dabbed at a tear gathering around her eyes. She turned to Nick who stood behind the cab waiting to be introduced. Gently placing her dark palm in the light skinned one, she greeted "you are welcome, *Americana*" with a huge smile. She felt the warm soft hand, winked at Stella and timidly retracted her hand. She embraced Stella again and took her by the hand. Mathew dragged the luggage inside the house to Stella's room.

The family sat down to eat at the long and wide dining table. The cutlery was neatly placed in the right corners and two-course meals were placed in the center of the table. Martha kept glancing at the huge standing clock in the living room. She allowed her eyes to be distracted by the pendulum on the huge clock as it oscillated with a loud *"chuck-chuck-chuck-chuck."* She returned her gaze to her husband

and asked, "Did you try his number again?" Chief Ndube sighed and stared at his wrist watch as if the huge clock was incorrect.

"Let's eat dear. Chike has never kept time in anything. I called him yesterday to accompany us to the airport and he promised he would meet us there. Did you see him there?" he retorted.

"No, I didn't," Martha replied sharply.

"You remember when I was calling his number on our way back from the airport to meet us at home but he didn't answer. Let's eat, *biko* — please. When he's done with his business deals, which always come before his family, then he can sneak in on us like a thief in the night," he said with a stern look.

He knew his son enough to not to trust him to be punctual. He knew Chike would show up when everything, every excitement, and good news had ended. With that, they began to eat Paulina's well-prepared dinner. Normally, Paulina would order the other maids to prepare meals for her boss and his wife. But on that day Stella arrived with her boyfriend, she took it upon herself to prepare the meal.

Nick who was still getting used to the foreign environment, unfamiliar family, and heavily spiced food kept searching the face of his girlfriend's father for clues. He waited for Stella to try the food first before he followed suit. He tried not to meet Chief Ndube's angrily-fixated eyes.

Her father deliberately wanted to make Nick uncomfortable, and who knows, the Chief thought, because of the intolerable ways of *white* people, Nick might just stand up and leave, never to return.

Stella noticed the way her father glared at her man. Noticing the tension in Nick's thighs when she placed her hand on them, she tapped him and whispered, "Don't worry about him, Sweetie." As much as Nick wanted to relax and enjoy the spicy meal, the wide, dark face with bulging eyes staring at his every move from the picking up of the spoon to the lowering of it, was awkward.

"Young man, how did you meet my daughter?" At last, the man seemed ready to have a normal conversation – a man to man conversation -- the type of conversation a father would have with his daughter's boyfriend, or so Nick thought.

"Well sir, we met during her internship in my father's company." Chief Ndube lifted his eyes off the smoothly pounded yam before him. Something in him was proud that his daughter didn't settle for less. At least it might be bearable to have a rich white boy as a son-in-law.

"Which company?" he queried.

"Dad, remember when I told you I did my internship at the diamond exchange in Toronto?" Stella interrupted hoping to save her lover from the embarrassing questioning.

"I am asking the man, not you," Chief Ndube hushed her without any expression on his face. With his eyes still fixated on Nick, like a dog trying to figure out his owner's next move, he asked "Diamonds must be a good business I suppose, but one can only wonder how you acquire them. Isn't it so?"

Nick nodded, trying to fathom what all was behind the question, and said, "Actually sir, this business has passed from generation to generation, from my grandfather, to my father, and to me. We have miners from whom we purchase the diamonds, and then they go into the full processes of polishing and registering before they make their way to the lovely fingers such as those of Mrs. Ndube, who enjoys wearing beautiful stones," Nick teased as he beamed at Martha.

Martha who had been listening to the interview the whole time couldn't help but smile at the boy's sense of humor. However, her husband wasn't sharing the humor at all. Rather he was more infuriated at the way the boy had twisted his response. He decided to try another ploy. Questioning was something he knew very well how to do, judging from the carefully chosen one-hundred employees on his payroll who had gone through a series of eyeball to eyeball questioning.

"You mean stealing from the miners, don't you?" This time Chief Ndube waited to judge the impact of his obnoxious choice of words.

"Dad, I think this question is getting out of hand," Stella interrupted. "Nick has barely touched his meal because you are just bombarding him with questions. He's not a thief. His father owns the biggest diamond exchange in Toronto. This was a business his father inherited from his grandfather. They've been in the business too long to have built their reputation by thievery!"

Paulina moved over to where Chief Ndube was sitting and collected the empty plates. Martha turned to her husband and said "Darling, let it be," and then changed the subject of the awkward conversation by turning to her daughter and asking, "*nne m* – my

dear, I hope you enjoyed the meal?"
Stella nodded and wiped her mouth with the table cloth. She turned to Paulina and said "Aunty, I've missed your cooking so much! It's been too many years."
Paulina smiled at her and then turned to Nick whose cheeks had turned pink from suppressing the surge of anger that rose in him. He had been calm the whole time at the table but he was no longer doing a good job in hiding it. To the rest of the family, it simply looked like he was suffering from the heat of the spicy goat meat he was chewing on.
"Americana, do you eat this kind of food in your country?" Paulina asked naively, smiling and revealing her stained teeth. It was a question asked only by those unacquainted with the rest of the world. She knew better than to ask him that, but there was a kind of satisfaction that came from hearing him speak his Canadian accent. It was as if he spoke with his nose. "No ma'am," Nick replied, "but I must commend you on the well prepared meal. I definitely enjoyed it."
Paulina giggled as she listened. She knew she couldn't repeat what he had just said, but it sounded good anyway. After dinner, Stella took Nick's hand and walked down the hallway leading to the living room.
As soon as Stella entered the spacious living room which was well decorated with cultural artifacts, she noticed her father glaring at her from the corner. Nick, still as clueless as a stranger in a strange land, stood aghast, watching as Chief Ndube pulled his daughter into his room. Burning in fury, he threw his

cap on the neatly made bed with floral sheets and light blanket folded at the edge. "Stella, if I didn't see that birth mark on your neck the moment you emerged from that arrival hall at the airport; if I didn't remember that little girl I used to lift to my shoulder, I would have said you were not my daughter." Stella pretended not to know where her father's talks were headed. Still, she listened on. "I am very disappointed in you. I sent you to Canada to study, and the best way to thank us your parents is to drag home a white boy?" By now, she was becoming impatient.

"Let him get straight to the point," she thought. Stella wiped off the sweat on her forehead as a result of the warm weather outside. She had just returned from a long and tiring journey and this reaction could have waited till tomorrow, she thought, but it wouldn't; it would be sorted out tonight by her father.

She had to speak, to contain this hatred before it succeeded. "Dad, where is all this coming from? I just got back, for God's sake. Can't we have this talk another time?"

With the words streaming out of her mouth, Chief Ndube felt like wrapping his large palms around her slender neck and squeezing till her eyes popped out of her skull. He had his resentment when it came to interracial marriages; he had his opinion when it came to deciding what happens in his family, but the two of them mixed together, the racial insult and the defiance, to come from his own daughter, there could be nothing peaceful about it.

"Did you tell me you were returning with a man?" He queried. "Did you even tell your mother about this stranger?" He barked.

"Dad I'm sorry I didn't mention him. Nick and I love each other. He insisted on meeting you. I love him, dad." Stella explained, but this only fueled her father's anger.

"What will your brother say when he hears this? What will my friends and colleagues say?" he queried. The rage in his heart made his eyes pink as if someone had punched them. He held tightly to the edge of the mahogany desk at the corner of the room. "What will your friends say?"

"Is that what you are mostly concerned about? Appearances? What everyone will think? How about what makes me happy?" Stella yelled. She knew her father's temper could get out of control. But before it did, she had to give him her piece of mind.

The argument continued, echoing into the hallway. Nick who was still standing in the hallway decided to sit on the couch in the waiting room. The argument was in Igbo language so the more he stretched his ears to grasp whatever the bone of contention was, the less he understood. As he sat and crossed his legs, with his left fist supporting his jaw, he reflected on why he had followed Stella down to her hometown. He came from a city where women would die to marry him; a world where he lacked nothing--where he had maids and secretaries listening to his every order and carrying them out swiftly without arguments; a world where he had money to throw-- where women vied with each other to be at his side. "What had he seen in Stella anyway? What was so extraordinary about Stella that made him abandon all that just to be with her?" he asked himself.

She was a young beautiful Nigerian woman with manners, humor and brains to top it all. He remembered vividly the first day she walked into his office dressed in a black skirt, white short sleeved shirt carrying a file in her hand. "Good morning," she had said. He had heard lots of good mornings from his colleagues, servants, and even his computer, on the radio when he was driving to work, but none of them got his attention the way that one came from this beautiful lady. Her eyes impressed him because they were so alert, aware, curious and, above all, shrewd. It was the day she began working in his company as an intern in Public Relations. This only made him think deeper about his recent experience; how could someone as beautiful and intelligent as she, be the tail end of a hateful man? As he wondered, he glanced at his Rolex wrist watch, the gift she had bought him on his twenty-ninth birthday.

Chapter 2

The door was flung open by a tall, light skinned man in a button shirt and trouser. Nick saw him from afar walking toward the living room. As he drew closer, his face became familiar to him. He gently stood up and moved a few inches from the couch he was sitting on to allow the young man see him clearly. He was very bad with names, especially African names, but he remembered the young man from college.

As soon as Chike saw the tall, blonde, Caucasian male with muscular arms in the navy blue shirt, he also knew he had seen that face before. If not, what would a white man be doing in his father's compound at that time of the night? He shouted "Nick?" then drew closer. "Nick is that you?" he asked again, this time face to face with him as he stood there with a huge smile, filled with surprise. "*Wassup mehn?* Where've you been?" Nick shouted throwing his arms around Chike.

"Nick Walsh, the diamond Nick?" Chike shouted for the third time as if no one had heard him before.

The two friends laughed for some time and slumped on the couch. As soon as Chike regained his mind, he asked "What in the world are you doing in Africa, in Nigeria?" Nick still smiling and gazing at his long lost friend with admiration shook his head in surprise. "Don't tell me you know this family." He said. "This is my house *mehn*. This is my dad's house. Are you here on business?"

Nick sat up and stared deep at his friend. He shifted

to the edge of the seat with his elbow on his knees then asked "Your dad? You mean Stella is your sister?" This was only getting interesting for him. It was as if presents filled with surprises were being unwrapped before him. Stella had mentioned her brother a few times, but not with details of the Chike he knew. The loud noise from the two men sent Martha, Stella, and Chief Ndube rushing to the living room. As soon as Stella saw her brother, she ran into his arms.

"Chike, I ga agbali knwusi agwa ojo gi a. O diro nma — Chike, you have to change this attitude of yours. It's not fair at all." Martha yelled. "How could you? How could you disappoint your father and I today, today of all days when your younger sister returned from abroad. Not even a phone call? We all waited for you at the dinner table." Martha continued.

"I'm sorry," Chike apologized. "I was caught up in this meeting that took all day. We just finalized the deal tonight. I couldn't leave."

"Baby girl, I'm sorry. I'm so sorry, but I'm here now, and I will make it up to you." He apologized to Stella who shrunk in his arms.

"I'm glad you are not dead somewhere as I'd imagined. I'm off to bed. See you all in the morning," Martha said and walked away. She turned and noticed her husband glaring at Nick. She went back and gently took his hand. "Let's go to bed darling," she pleaded softly. With that, they disappeared in the hallway.

Chike turned to his friend still smiling, and then he looked at his younger sister and tickled her cheeks.

"So you know this bad boy here huh?" Stella fended

off her brother and went to sit on Nick's lap. She leaned closer and planted a kiss on his lips, and then turned her gaze to her brother who was bewildered at the sight of his sister kissing this man before him.

"You know each other?" she asked, staring at Nick quizzically.

"We don't just know each other; we lived together for years in the frat house. We lost contact after graduation." Nick explained.

"What a small world." Stella concluded.

"Okay bro, we have to go to bed now. It was a long flight." She stood up and took Nick's hand, leading him to her bedroom. Chike stood up and climbed the stairs leading to his bedroom.

As soon as Martha dozed off, her husband gently slipped out of bed, put on his slippers and walked down the hall to Stella's room. He tiptoed to the door and placed his ear gently on it. He frowned at the sound of kisses coming from the room, so he quickly opened the door and turned on the light switch. The bright light from the 60 watt bulb blinded Nick who hid his face in the pillow.

"Get up!" Chief Ndube barked frowning at his daughter.

"Dad, what is the meaning of this?" Stella asked angrily.

"Shut up. I am not talking to you. Young man, get up!" he commanded.

Nick got up confused and picked up his shirt which was lying on the floor, which had thrown off while Stella was caressing his body.

"Didn't your family raise you well? How dare you touch my daughter under my own roof? Get out! Go upstairs and sleep in Chike's room. I won't tolerate this in my house." Nick put his shirt on and walked towards the door.

"Hold on Nick. Dad, you are harassing my boyfriend. This is not fair. What has he done to you? Ever since we arrived, you've just been on his case. Why can't you just let him be?" Stella pleaded with her angry father who was already leaving the room.

As Nick stood by the side of the man, he measured how short he was. "Short and ugly," he muttered and scuffed. He climbed the stairs to Chike's room with Chief Ndube's eyes watching him to make sure he didn't slip back into his daughter's room. Chike opened the door and saw his friend staring at him with anger all over his face. He peered through him to see if his sister was coming too. "What's the matter, *mehn?*" Chike asked.

"Fuck, I'm tired of this shit. I can't believe this. Your dad is unbelievable," Nick cursed angrily.

"What happened?" Chike asked.

"He just busted into your sister's room and ordered me out saying he didn't want us to sleep together. Seriously?"

Nick laughed out loud saying "I'm sorry, *mehn.* That's African folks for you. Chill! You know what? Let's sleep. I'll talk to him in the morning."

"This isn't funny, Chike. I felt humiliated," Nick continued to complain.

"I know how you feel. I apologize okay," Chike said as he continued to laugh.

Nick stared at him, doubting the sincerity of his apologies.

"You are officially welcomed to the Ndube's family."

The next day was a busy one as the family gathered for their annual celebration. The servants wiped, swept, dusted, and tidied every corner of the house. This family tradition had started many years ago when the Senior Ndube handed his company over to his succeeding son, Chief Ndube, taking it upon himself to start a new tradition. So there was lots of food and drink for all.

While everyone was busy preparing for the party, Nick rested in bed and refused to dress up for the party. Stella who was already dressed in a red ballroom gown with a shiny patent clutch bag went to her brother's room and found Nick lying down. He was reading a book he had purchased at the duty-free store in Germany on their way from Canada. Surprised, she walked around the bed to a position where she could see his face.

"Honey, you aren't dressed yet? I thought Chike said you were preparing for the party."

Nick gently dropped the book, rubbed his shabby blonde hair and stared at her seductively. "Come here," he flirted with Stella.

"Didn't you hear me?" Stella asked again, ignoring his flirtatious stare.

"I did, but I can't find the right word to say to this beautiful lady standing before me. I can't even think. I just want to rip that dress off you," he replied.

Stella smiled, knowing where this conversation was headed, but she wasn't ready for that just yet.

"C'mon," she said. "We need to go to the party. If this is because of my dad, I already told you not to mind him; he's just overwhelmed that I have a boyfriend." Nick stared at her from the corner of his eyes and sighed.

"You want me to go and face another round of dinner table embarrassment? You know the only reason I am here is because of you. I love you, and nothing will ever change that."

Hearing those words from Nick made her smile and she wiggled her toes in the black leather heels she was wearing. She sat on the bed and shifted closer to him saying, "I know. I am sorry for yesterday's, today's and future embarrassments or insults he may give you. Please ignore him. If you run away from him, he will question your guts as a man. You need to prove to him that you take his words with a grain of salt."

Nick sat up and kissed her on the lips and then pecked her cheeks. He took her hands and squeezed them gently. Staring into her eyes, he acquiesced. "I'll go with you. Let me dress up."

Stella smiled again and stroked his hair. As he rose up to dress, she pulled her wide dress together.

Soon Nick was dressed in a ruby red long-sleeved shirt and a dark grey trouser. He parted his hair; one side brushed backwards and the other to the side. This made him look more like a gentleman than the man-child to which her father had reduced him. His blue eyes glittered in the bright light as he led his woman down to the large hall where the party was being held.

Immediately, when they walked into the crowded room, everyone turned to stare. Single ladies standing around without a partner beamed at Nick as he stood at the corner of the room with his right hand in the pocket, nervous from the staring crowd. This was the kind of stare people gave to a surprise guest. He was a white man in the crowded party filled with natives. Their eyes inquired as they snooped at him as if he was this alien that had lost his way. Chief Nwigwe who was standing with his friend Professor Sunday couldn't take his eyes off the young man.

Chief Ndube found himself jealous of Nick. He admired his patience, poise and good looks. But this enormity, this ancient grudge that had kept him away from accepting his future son in-law was powerful. He needed to frustrate him at every given opportunity. "Is that the boy?" Professor Sunday asked as he peered at Nick standing with Stella in the far corner of the room. Chief Ndube pretended not to have heard him. "He is good looking compared to others I've met." Professor Sunday rambled on without noticing his friend's countenance. Chief Ndube slipped away from him immediately as he saw Stella coming in their direction. He didn't want his friends to feel his thoughts about Nick.

Stella went to greet Professor Sunday when she saw him across the room. She left Nick in the company of her brother who was chatting with a group of friends. As she walked closer to Professor Sunday, she smiled and spread her arms to hug him. Sunday moved closer and hugged her gently. He was a short, bald-headed man with a voice that echoed like a girl's. He was well known for his proper use of grammar and often spoke like a literature professor, which is why he was called the Professor.

"Stella, Stella!" Professor Sunday called out to Stella who was smiling at him.

"How have you been, sir?" she asked.

"My dear, my weak bones have permitted me another

precious day," he replied.

"How are Nkechi and Uche?" she inquired.

"They are very well my dear. They couldn't make it. Nkechi just delivered a baby girl last week, and Uche is still doing his youth service" he explained. Stella was satisfied with the response he gave. They chatted a little further and then parted. The party started off with a floor dance. Everyone except the maids were invited to the dance floor with their partners, and followed by dinner.

As the guests sat before the long dinner table, with the hosts at the upper end of the table, a brief speech followed. "Ladies and gentlemen, can you all raise your glasses and let us toast to a fruitful year, a friendly year and many more years to come." The guests all lifted their glasses. Soon the room was filled with loud laughter and clinking glasses. After the toast, everyone settled back to their seats. The maids appeared with piping hot trays laden with rice, fried meats, soups and stews and began dishing it out to everyone at the table.

Everyone ate and conversed. Then Chief Ndube began, "May I have your attention again, ladies, gentlemen?" everyone lifted their faces and turned to listen to his announcement. "This year has been a fruitful year for us all; Ndube and Sons jewelry, our colleagues, staff and everyone gathered here today. Many years ago my late father handed over this company to me, and as a novice, I didn't know what to do with it. It was through your support and commitment that this company came to be what it is today. I also want to welcome my daughter back home. She has come to contribute the knowledge she learned abroad, so I encourage you all, my team and staff, to help her familiarize herself with this company.

I therefore propose a toast; to my friends, my families, and colleagues. Thank you for honoring this invitation. Have fun." His guests toasted and clapped. The laughter and chatter continued. Chike who had been quiet the whole time turned to his mother and said "Mum, this meal is very delicious. Don't tell me you never gave Aunty Paulina your recipe. Martha smiled at her son and said "Of course not. I do not want my son to mistake his mother's meal." They laughed.

Chief Ndube turned to his wife and said "Darling, you see what I was telling you at the airport? Anybody who grew up in this soil and ate this food of ours shall always return for more. Look at Chike; he lived in Canada for years and returned and yet he still never forgot how our food tasted." Martha smiled, ignoring her husband once again, and turned to her daughter and Nick who were seating adjacent to her saying, "my dear, please explain to your father very well about interracial marriage because I know that's where this talk is leading to. We argued about this earlier while at the airport, and now he wants to start again."

Nick looked at Chief Ndube and their eyes met. He shifted his gaze to his girlfriend. He knew where their talks were leading to but listened on. Professor Sunday chipped in, "my friend has said it all. A good meal like this will never permit a real man to perish in an unknown land. One must return for more." Stella turned to her father who just swallowed a mouthful of pounded yam which sent his eyes popping forward as the smooth and roundly molded dough glided down his throat, "so dad, what is the problem with interracial marriage?" Stella asked as she swallowed a small ball of pounded yam glazed in *ogbono* soup.

"There's no *problem o*. I was just pointing out to your mother the importance of a man marrying a Nigerian woman who can make meals like this one." Chief Ndube explained deftly as he licked the dripping soup off his fingers, hoping that this time, his daughter would support him. His eyes taunted Nick who scooped fried rice into his mouth.

"So what you are saying now is that if Chike had returned from Canada with a *white* woman, you will not allow him to marry her simply because she can't make *ogbono* soup?" Stella asked. Chike waited to hear what his father would say. Of course he knew his father's principles when it came to interracial marriages, but the way he would say it would be far more interesting that the principle itself.

Chapter 3

Chief Ndube felt a harsh sting at the mentioning of marriage. All the while, he had been careful not to reveal the main reason for his controversial opinion about white people to his family.

"Chike is the son of his father. He will not try it. He will never ever try it. No son of mine shall rub my mouth in the mud," he defended.

"But what if he does?" Stella maintained.

"Alright, let's not stress ourselves with this issue. Stella, your brother has finalized his marriage plans with Agatha." Martha said cheerfully, hoping that the argument doesn't continue.

On hearing that, Stella turned to her brother who looked shy and winked at her.   But Professor Sunday has always enjoyed his friend's conversation and wanted to hear more, so he encouraged the debate.

 "I hear they don't even eat any heavy meal. How is a man to survive in that country without *fufu* — pounded yam or the likes?" he asked and waited for someone to follow up on the topic.

Stella knew this wasn't the first time she'd heard Professor Sunday and her father discuss white people. She turned to her boyfriend who was just listening and sipping his drink and rubbed his shoulder, smiling.

"Stella," the chief began, "let me explain something to you. I lived in Washington D.C for eight years before I moved to Los Angeles. I hadn't even met your mum then. Now I'm sure you know that those are big cities in the US in those days, and I saw a lot of things too. All I'm saying is that we have to preserve our culture, our *Omenala*. Now if every man in this country settles for white women, we will have a country filled with colored babies and none of them will be able to speak their language let alone maintain the tradition." Chief Ndube continued, determined to make his point. This pained Martha the more that her educated husband reasoned like an illiterate at times. They were still in the conversation when the gateman escorted someone to the dining table. The stranger was a photographer whom Chief Ndube had paid to enhance an old photograph he found in his father's room after he died. The photographer promised to bring the grainy, sepia-colored photograph back to life. It was on that day that Chief Ndube had thought of a better strategy to get rid of the white man that had made his way into his house.

As soon as Chief Ndube waived at the gateman, he moved swiftly back to his post. The photographer stood and waited to be spoken to before he could speak. "What took you so long? I planned to present it as a surprise to my family and employees earlier during my speech, but you weren't here." Chief Ndube asked the photographer, and the eyes of the entire family stared at him while still gobbling their meal.

"Sorry sir. I was held up in traffic. I tried to get here as quick as I could. Nevertheless, I have fixed the picture as you requested, and you will barely notice the odd shape of it as I framed it equally." He revealed a large squared wooden frame, revealing the face of two young men — a young, white man hugging a young black man.

As the photographer lifted the frame to Chief Ndube's view, the chief's eyes widened in excitement. A teardrop gathered round his eyes. Ignoring it, he stood up, wiped his hand with the napkin on the table and took the frame from the photographer. He stared at it with so much glee, and then walked straight to the wide cream-painted wall and hung it loosely on the wall. He moved back a couple of inches to observe the balance, and then went back to position it properly. He walked back to the table without a word and caught his wife staring at him pitifully. He tried to spread a smile around and resume his conversation, but one could see that he was no longer in the mood for a racial debate.

Chike, noticing his father's mood, stood and walked over to the photographer. He placed one arm on the man's shoulder and whispered into his ears. The man nodded, picked up the wrapper littered on the floor and left the room. As the room regained its silence, something caught Nick's eyes on the frame. He had been trying to figure out who the people in the photo are and why Chief Ndube was sad. He gently stood up and walked towards the wall where the frame was hung. He stood there for a minute and stared at the faces. He didn't recognize the black man's face, but judging from their faces, something told him that it was either Chief Ndube's brother or father. He returned his gaze to the white man. He recognized him. He had seen a picture like that in his father's album back in Toronto.

It was his grandfather who was in the frame with

Chief Ndube's father. He chuckled and turned to look at the family who were now staring at his back as if they were waiting for him to make a judgment on the photo. Out of impatience, Chike said "That's my grandfather with his friend back in the day." As if Nick didn't hear him, he continued to stare at the picture and said "I think this is my grandfather in the picture. This is so interesting! I didn't know he had been here before. I never met him though. Those are really some miner boots he had on there." As soon as he mentioned 'grandfather', everyone's mouth slipped open in horror.

He continued to speak as he remained turned away from the family. Chief Ndube turned furiously and stood up again from his chair. He walked over to where Nick was still standing and observing the photo. With anger all over his face, he gently asked "Did you say this man, Mr. Walter, is your grandfather?" Nick turned around to face him. Sensing the anger in his voice, he took a step backward and replied, "Yes. I think that's him. Grandpa Walter."

Professor Sunday who was also enjoying the argument didn't want it to stop, "This is interesting! Is that to say that he has come to take what his grandfather left behind?" he asked. Chief Ndube drew a long breath, turned to his family on the table, turning his eyes to his daughter, glaring at her. He returned his now red eyes again to Nick and barked "Quietly go into that room, pack your things and get out of my house." Stella jumped out of the table and ran over to her father. Confused as to why he would yell at Nick like that, she queried, "Dad what is going on here? He only identified the man as his grandfather. What's the crime there? Dad do you know what time it is? He came here with me. You just can't throw him out."

Martha got up and went over to where her husband, Nick, and Stella were standing. She angrily grabbed her hand and pulled her away from Nick's grip saying, "You don't understand a thing, child. Go and have a seat!" Stella more confused and anxious as to what was happening, ran over to where Nick was standing bemused as well and held his shoulder asking, "baby what is going on here?" Nick shrugged and continued to stare at Chief Ndube. Chike stood up and walked over to his father and whispered something into his ears and waited for his response. Chief Ndube stared at him with anger and walked away. Chike walked behind him to his room.

Everyone left quietly except Paulina who was left to clean up the dishes. As Stella and Nick walked a few feet away from the messy dining table, she watched Paulina gently gathering the china wares to the kitchen. She has also noticed her man's mood but knew a discussion wouldn't solve it. Everyone needed to be quiet. She walked back to the table and began picking up the cutlery and followed Paulina to the kitchen. Nick walked up the stairs leading to Chike's room where he sleeps.

Paulina was happy to see her, but didn't want her in the kitchen. "*Nne m*, please don't stress yourself. Go to your room, we will chat tomorrow." Paulina urged. "Aunty, please don't tell me to go away. What is going on with my family? Why is everyone acting weird tonight?" Stella queried with a frown on her face.

"I suggest you ask your father. He will explain to you better. Please make sure this young man is safe and make him leave here before things grow worse." Again, puzzled and anxious for an answer, she walked over to Paulina and asked, "Aunty, I need you to tell me what is going on. What has this young man done to my father in these couple of days that I'm not aware of?" Paulina walked away from her and continued to clean the dining table, then said, "Before it was just his color, but today it's his grandfather. Something happened. Go to your father..."

Stella stood there staring at her and then walked away. When she didn't see Nick in the hallway where she left him, she dashed into her father's room and found Chief Ndube sitting on the edge of the bed with Chike and her mother deliberating something. Feeling left out of the secret, she went and knelt before her father with tears in her eyes. She allowed the first drop of tears to land on her father's knees before she spoke, "Dad, what is going on? Why are you all hurting me like this? Is it because he's white? Is it because he's not the son of your business associate? Is that the reason for all these hatred?" She then wiped off the tears with the hem of her dress. Chief Ndube stared at her and gently moved her away from his knees. He stood up, with his hands behind him, he said, "What I am about to tell you is something very painful and unforgivable. I want you to listen carefully so you will understand why we feel this way. That young man you brought here is a curse to this family. Chike rubbed his thin beard and listened with so much interest as if he was hearing the story for the first time.

"In 1944, a group of men who claimed that they were business men came to the village in search of a trade," Chief Ndube began, "My father, your grandfather was only a young man who didn't understand the white man's mission. He met Walter and they became close friends. Your grandfather knew that their friendship was only for a short period. It would end as soon as he returned to Canada. He told me how Walter promised to take him to Canada, and how they would become roommates in school."

Stella listened attentively but wondered in her mind what this story had to do with his boyfriend. She cut her father off by asking, "So dad, does this story have anything to do with Nick?" Chief Ndube glared at her for two reasons, first for interrupting him, and secondly for not waiting to hear the end of the story so she could agree with him. "Stella, if you would let me finish, then you'll know why I despise your so-called lover."

Stella turned around to see her brother's expressionless face. Something was really going on and she had no idea where or how to catch up. She turned to her mother who quickly moved her face.

"Dad, I don't care what his family did to you, but Nick is not a thief! He's educated, honest, and he's rich and manages a multi-million dollar company. He has nothing to do with this." As she rambled, Chief Ndube moved his face. "You'll like him once you get to know him. I love him papa, I do." She pleaded.

"That fool will never be a part of this family! He must leave first thing in the morning. I don't want to ever see you with him again. This family will not tolerate such!" he barked.

"If he leaves, I'm going with him. You either accept him for my sake or I go back to Canada with him!" Stella threatened with an air of finality. On hearing this, Chike glanced at his father who signaled him and he dashed out of the room. "I'm sorry child; I won't let you leave with that thief. He's no good for you. He's not your type and there's no place for the both of you in this family."

Stella ran after Chike who was now rummaging through her luggage with her clothes littered on the floor of her room and her passport in his hand. He frowned at her and made for the door. She ran after him and struggled to get the passport from him but Chike's manly arms were no match for her as he dashed back into their father's room and handed it to him. Stella stood there staring angrily at her father and Chike, feeling so helpless. All she could do was cry.

Chapter 4

As Chief Ndube was telling his story, Nick was now in Chike's room wondering what the discussion was about. Stella told him to wait so she could speak to her father, but what exactly was he waiting for? His eyes caught the *Ife* art carving on the wall; it was a wooden face of a man with a hole in it. From afar, it looked like a man screaming out loud without a noise.

Nick stared at the art for a while then brought his head closer and deeper into the hollow mouth of the carving. He peered into it like a dentist in search of cavity. He wondered at first how many days it took the carver to smooth the hole which appeared to be a mouth, and what was going on in the carver's head. That's the type of question one would ask Michelangelo--what he was thinking when he painted the Sistine chapel. In anxiety, he brought out his cell phone which was lying in his pocket and began punching in some numbers. He brought it close to his ear and waited. A voice came up and spoke in a gentle and groggy "hello," Nick rubbed his face and gently rubbed his blonde hair backwards. "It's me. You sound like you've not been taking your medications." Nick said. "How is it over there in Africa?" the voice asked. He breathed into the phone and sat down at the edge of the bed and said "I'll be returning soon. There seems to be a bit of a mix up somewhere." The voice spoke louder this time as if it just woke up from a sleep. "What about the stones? You got them with you?" Nick rubbed his head again, rolled his eyes slowly upwards and then focused his gaze at his shoe. "Not really. As a matter of fact, things seem to be going off plan." The voice was silent for a few seconds and then hung up. He glanced at the phone and saw that the call had ended. He threw it on the bed angrily. He hated when his father hung up on him unannounced.

The door opened, and there stood Stella, her face covered in tears. She walked a few feet towards Nick and grabbed his hand. She kissed it gently and lifted her face to meet his eyes. He wondered what the verdict was this time being that he has never seen his girlfriend that emotional before. He wanted to ask what happened to her while talking to her father, but it was better to allow her download her mind gently. The sight of her sobbing was unbearable for him. Quickly, he took out his blue and white, rumpled, handkerchief and began soaking the tears away from her cheeks.

"Sit down," she said, pointing at the bed a few feet away from them. "Baby, what is the matter now? I told you it was a bad idea to have returned here after such a long time. Your family doesn't understand you; they do not notice the change in you. What have they said to you this time?" He consoled her.

"Do you remember the first time we went on a date?" Stella asked him. "You said something to me; you said that whatever will be, will be." she said gently with her right arm on his shoulder.

Nick cogitated on the meaning of her words. He remembered vividly what he said to her, but of what use was it at that moment? He wondered. "What is the matter?" he asked.

"Dad told me everything. He's really bitter about it and I suggest you go back to Canada until everything is sorted out. At this time Nick's perplexity set in. "Aren't you coming with me?"

"Aren't you interested in knowing why?" Stella retorted angrily. Nick realized how unconcerned he'd been for not asking the most important question at that time. "I'm sorry, what happened? What is bothering your father?" he asked scornfully.

"As I was saying, whatever that happens between us, if we can overcome it, we will definitely be together. We have a bigger problem ahead of us and only our love can conquer it. I need you to promise me something," she pleaded.

Nick, on hearing the word promise, got apprehensive. *Why was she putting off the main story and what else was he to promise her*? He promised to love her which he did; He promised to follow her to Africa which he fulfilled, and he even promised to ignore her father's attitude towards him, so what else does she want? "Promise you what baby, promise you what?" he probed desperately, searching her round brown eyes.

"Promise me that we will get through this together, that you will be there no matter what happens." She continued, still staring deep into his eyes. "Okay, tell me what you are driving at. I am getting impatient." Nick interrupted. Truly, he was getting impatient. He needed everything laid out for him so he could plan his next move.

"Your grandfather stole from my grandfather sixty-eight years ago!" She dropped. Nick's eyes widened and his mouth too heavy to speak, he sprung out of bed and walked away from her. "What?" escaped his mouth as he stared down at her. His heart began pounding faster and light sweat gathered at the nape of his neck.

"Yes you heard me. That's why my father wants you to leave. That also explains his hatred for white people." Stella explained.

"But sixty-eight years is a long time to hold grudge on someone and his progeny. Did you tell him we are in love? Perhaps that would soften his heart?" Nick asked with a positive anticipation. "He doesn't want to see you now, Nick. I think the best thing is for you to go back to Canada, and then we can figure it out slowly." Stella replied weakly without looking at him. She was heartbroken at the news and had no place for a decent decision at that moment. Nick banged his hands on the wooden table angrily and cursed out loud.

Her eyes were now fixated on the same carving on the wall which Nick had been staring at before she walked in. "You will come with me then?" Nick asked suggestively, but on searching Stella's face, he realized she wasn't going to do so but still posed the question.

"Sweetie, I'm asking you, are you coming with me to Canada or not?"

Stella lifted her face to look at his now pink cheeks. It was obvious he was angry at the way things were turning out for him. He watched another teardrop escape her eye as she spoke, "Nick, I think you should go for now. I'll stay behind to sort out this issue. I will keep you posted." Stella replied, got up and went to kiss him, but he turned his face away. "What do you mean by that?

"I wish I could Nick, but…"

"But what, baby?"

"They snatched my passport from me. They won't let me go with you." Stella dropped.

In the wee hours of the morning, Mathew the driver was already waiting for Nick to take him to the airport. The sudden discovery had circulated in the entire household that even the maids saw him as the unlucky suitor. He quietly rolled his *echolac* suitcase into the trunk of the black Honda civic waiting for him. He sat at the back of the car and without a word, and Mathew rolled out of the compound.

As they drove towards the airport, Mathew kept glancing at the rear view mirror as if he was instructed to watch what Nick was doing. He couldn't hold his curiosity any longer that he asked in his rather ridiculous ascent in *Pidgin* English, "*Oga Rick, ayam vely soli o.* -Mr. Nick I am very sorry." Nick was too lost in thought to hear him but something made him look into the rear view mirror, and he caught Mathew's eyes staring at him. "Pardon?" Nick asked. Mathew smiled wholeheartedly on hearing the white man speak to him. He muttered the word 'pardon' a couple of times to himself as if to memorize it.

He pulled over to the side of the road and parked the car. He turned around fully, facing Nick, with a smile and said, "*I know say you dey mad, bur madam too dey mad. I say make una take evely thing easy o*---I know you and madam (Stella) are both angry, so please take it easy." He advised innocently with a full smile on his lips which revealed a light brown pigmentation on his lower lip from his smoking habit.

Nick didn't understand what the man said but the frequent use of the word "angry" got him uninterested in whatever he had to say. "*I hear wetin your grandpapa do to oga papa. Oga Rick, tru-tru e no good o. How man go steal from another man and fiam! disappear like that, like a thief in the night? Aya m vely shur say na the thing kill the man sef.*---I heard about the story about what your grandfather did and honestly I think it wasn't fair. How could a man steal from another man and disappear without a trace? I'm sure that must have killed Stella's grandfather." Mathew continued to converse in Pidgin English without catching the expression on Nick's face.

Nick on hearing the word 'grandfather' and 'steal', quickly got an idea of what the driver was saying. A surge of anger crossed his heart and he began staring at the man in a way to shut him up and keep driving, but Mathew was far too gone in his own discussion. He rambled on. It was not until Nick barked at him to drive that he quickly fished out the car key he had thrown into his blue and grey plaid shirt pocket, and started the car. He zoomed off with a frown on his face and thought about what he had just said to the man who seemed not to understand a word.

At a point, he began feeling pity for Nick whose face was clouded in anger. The car pulled in front of Murtala Mohammed International Airport. Nick peered out and looked at the high airport tower then brought his head back into the car and saw Mathew staring at him."*Oga, we don reach.*—Sir, we've arrived." That was the only decent comment he knew he could throw at Nick's way at that moment

Nick got out and waited for Mathew to come and

unload the trunk. Soon, a young boy about 16 years-old ran to them with a luggage cart shouting, "*Oga,* I will push it. Let me take it." The boy spoke quickly, running over to help Mathew bring out the luggage and into the cart. Nick stepped backward and watched as the men placed his luggage gently on the cart, then the boy hustled the cart into the airport. Nick turned to Mathew, brought out his wallet and picked out two hundred dollar notes and gave to him. Mathew smiled broadly and bowed to greet him. He patted the money on his sweaty fore-head and then squeezed it into his khaki shorts. "*Oga, e go better.* — It shall be well. *Na when you go come back to see us again?* — when will you come to visit us again?" Nick thought about the question but had no answer for the driver.

With his face clueless, Nick smiled and said, "Soon…" Then he walked into the airport to meet the boy already waiting for him at the check-in stand with his eyes staring at Nick's wallet bulging from his fitted jeans pocket. He brought out the wallet again and handed the boy a fifty-dollar bill. The boy smiled and disappeared before Nick could change his mind.

Chapter 5

Stella had been in her room crying all morning. Nick had left without saying goodbye. She knew he was angry. On top of it all, being denied the right to leave with him when she knew she needed to, killed her even more. As she stood beside her queen sized bed, she kept staring at her phone, contemplating whether or not to call him. As she dropped her phone on her bed, she ran to her father's room to confront him. Someone needed to take the heat from her. Forgetting to knock, she pushed the door ajar and found her father reading on his computer and her mother still in bed. "Where are your manners, child?" her father barked. "Dad, he left! He left…Are you happy now? You've finally sent him away." She lamented. "Good riddance to bad rubbish!" The man retorted and returned his gaze at his computer screen. "Is that why you barged into my room like that? Lest I forget, Chief Nwigwe's oldest son, Obike, your childhood friend, is returning to the country in two days. He has invited us to the welcoming party. That's a good boy with good manners. Now you must cheer up. You must look your best," he continued, undaunted.

"Dad, why are you doing this? You don't even care about my own happiness. Have you even asked me what I want?" Stella continued, ignoring her father's decoy of distraction.

"I am your father and I do not need to ask you what you want. I already know it. You are only a child and soon you will forget all about that boy. No child of mine will marry from a family of thieves. Thank your stars I didn't have him arrested."

Stella stood at the door with mouth wide open as her father condemned her lover. "I do not wish to discuss this issue anymore. There are a million and one men in the world that can make you happy besides that boy." He continued still not looking up to his daughter. "I do not want a million and one men, daddy," she retorted. "I want Nick. I love him." Martha who was awakened by the noise got up and went to her daughter. Glaring at her husband whose favorite hobby was to prove stubborn in every situation asked, "What is it this time, Chief? Why are you hurting this girl?" Chief Ndube looked at her from the corner of his eyes and stood up.

"I have done nothing to her. We need to be sensible here. You and I know how I feel about that boy. I didn't even know his true identity, and I already hated him. Now he has turned out to be the son of a thief, and you stand there to ask me what I did to her?" he defended himself.

"Mum, Nick left. He's gone!" Stella complained to Martha, sobbing as if she could bring him back with magic. "We had a fight last night. I asked him about everything. He didn't even know about the stolen diamond. I asked him to leave since dad threatened him. Now he's gone." Martha, glaring at her husband again, took Stella's hand and walked out of the room to Stella's.

After checking in his luggage, Nick realized he still had one hour before boarding the plane. Walking past the crowded and noisy airport filled with passengers negotiating with airlines about their over-sized luggage, he took the escalator to the restaurant. As he sat down in the open restaurant, he brought out his phone and stared at it for a few seconds deliberating whether to call Stella or not. He finally beat his pride and dialed her number. He brought the phone to his ear gradually and listened as it dialed, but there was no response. Disappointed, he dropped the phone on the table and picked up the restaurant menu on the table before him. Disgruntled, he waived at the waiter to attend to him.

As Martha and Stella sat down on the bed, Martha stared at her sad daughter with pity. "Have you called him yet?" she inquired. Stella shook her head.

"No. I don't know if he will even pick up my calls. He may feel abandoned. I brought him here, and then I sent him away." Stella winced and wheezed while Martha listened. Noticing the clear mucus traveling down Stella's lips, Martha quickly grabbed a tissue from the table and wiped it off, then returned her gaze to her daughter. Stella collected another sheet of soft tissue and soaked her tears. "Well, give him time, and then call him later to see if he arrived home safely," Martha advised.

"Love is tough my dear, and there's no better way to follow it than to have patience. Your father has never stopped talking about the man who stole his father's diamonds ever since we got married. I was up all night discussing this issue with him; to forgive and let you both be. As you can see, he's very stubborn. He will only do that which he sets his mind to do." Martha continued, "All I can tell you is to be patient with him. With time, he will understand. Okay?" she consoled her daughter. "Let me go and get ready. I have a meeting with my distributors this morning. We will talk more when I return. I will instruct Paulina to bring your breakfast. *I nula, nwa m ebezina.* — stop crying my dear." She said, stood up, and left the room.

Stella slumped on her bed and reached for her cell phone. She noticed that Nick had called her twice when she was in her father's room. She tried to redial the number but it was switched off. He might have already boarded the plane. Soon there was a loud knock on the door to her room. She waited to hear the knock again. Chike walked in with pity on his face. "What do you want?" She asked, before he could announce his reason for coming to her room.

"How are you holding up?" he asked, ignoring her first comment.

"I am well. You and dad conspired to send him away. I thought he was your friend, your college roommate. Why didn't you beg dad? Why didn't you even try to resolve the matter? Rather you supported your father. Now he's gone. I hope you are happy," she lamented. Chike noticed how angry his sister was and went to where she was lying on the bed. He placed his hand on her shoulder saying, "I am sorry, sis. He wronged our family and I don't expect dad to just ignore everything. I only reasoned with him. I am sorry about how you feel, but this is a family matter versus your emotions. You especially can't marry someone whose family has hurt us. There was no way I would have allowed you to run away with him," Chike advised.

To Stella, everyone was only interested in what Nick's

grandfather did, not about her own feelings. A surge of anger and hatred crossed her face as she glowered at her brother. She stood up from the bed and walked into the bathroom, avoiding further discussions.

A few minutes after Nick landed in Toronto Pearson airport, he noticed his personal driver waiting for him outside. Dressed in a white tuxedo shirt and a black suit, the middle aged man waved cheerfully at Nick. Spotting his luggage, he went to help Nick load it into the waiting car. Without a word, Nick abandoned his luggage for the man and went to sit inside the cozy black Cadillac sedan. He fished out his Blackberry phone, inserted his Canadian sim card, and began punching in some numbers. He waited for a voice to come on.

"Hello," a voice spoke.

"I'm on my way home. Are you already at the office?" Nick inquired and waited for a response. "No. I was waiting for the Diamond cutter. He called to reschedule so I may be here for a few minutes," the voice answered. "Ok. Wait for me then. I have something to talk to you about." Nick concluded the call. He placed the phone on his lap and turned to see if the driver was finished loading his bags in the trunk.

Soon the door was opened and the driver got in with a smile saying, "How was your trip, sir?" He started the car and waited for a response.

"It could have been better…" Nick replied weakly. "Drive to my dad's house first, I need to see him," he said, avoiding further questions from the driver. He had been his long-term driver and his closest friend. The driver had worked for his father long before he joined him.

"Didn't Miss Stella return with you?" The man resumed his query.

"Who?" Nick replied angrily as if he didn't hear him at first.

"I meant Stella," the man answered cheerfully. Nick ignored the man's question. Stella wasn't the discussion for the day. There were far more pressing issues than discussing Stella, he thought, then supported his jaw with his left fist as he engaged in a long thought. The car sped through the wide, clean road.

As soon as Mathew returned from the car wash and entered the living room to drop the car key, Stella rushed after him curiously.

''Mattie?" Mattie was more of a pet name everyone called the slow driver. "Did Nick say anything to you yesterday on your way to the airport?" she asked. Mathew scratched his head with the key and replied in Pidgin English "Small madam, you mean *Oga Rick*? – "Madam, are you talking about Nick?" Mathew remembered that the large amount of money Nick gave him yesterday, when converted to naira notes, would be equivalent to his six-month' salary. "Yes, I mean Nick, not Rick!" She retorted angrily, again. This man was annoying her with his stupid questions and responses. *By the way, why does he call him Rick, when Nick was easy to pronounce?* She wondered.

"*Eh, Oga Rick, sorry didn't spoken a word to me as we wented to the airport. The man just dey think, dey think,--*He didn't say a word to me on our way to the airport. He looked worried all through," he narrated trying so hard to impress his boss's daughter who had just returned from abroad, while he drifted away from the question.

"Thinking about what?" she interrupted him, bursting her impatience. "*I no know o…he just sidon dey think. Then he gif me oyibo dollars.* — I don't know what he was thinking about but he gave me some dollars anyway." The man rambled in Pidgin English. Disgruntled at Mathew's idiotic response, Stella quickly brushed past him and went into the kitchen. She had expected him to give her a clue about Nick's feelings as he drove him to the airport, but the token she was given left a better impression on her mind that Nick was also worried about the state of things. As she opened the refrigerator that revealed neatly arranged drinks, leftover meals, and vegetables, she bent to peep inside hoping to find something interesting. She reached out for the flavored milk which was hidden behind one of the Ziploc containers. Lifting it, she check for the expiration date, opened it and sniffed it. She then took a sip, allowing the chilled beverage to travel down her throat. As she sipped more from the white bottle, she couldn't stop thinking about her boyfriend. Why are things suddenly turning sore all of a sudden? This was the man she loved; the man who had followed her all the way from Canada to West Africa leaving behind his life, his empire, his family and friends just to be with her. With this tempter bubbling in her heart, she quickly gulped down the remaining fluid in the bottle, dumped it into the trash and stormed out of the kitchen.

Chapter 6

The black Cadillac gently pulled before a cream colored mansion with a statue of cupid in the fountain. The building, when gazed at from the left, was in the shape of a triangle. One couldn't fathom what Mr. Walsh had in mind when he chose the design. As soon as the tall and muscular body guard at the main door noticed Nick's car, he quickly walked to the passenger side and opened the door gently with a bow. Nick stepped out, adjusted his shirt and headed for the main door without a word to the man or to the driver who stared at his back as he marched.

As he opened the living room door, he took off his bronzed-lens sunglasses and glanced around the ornately furnished living room. He walked towards the wide staircase with curved, silver handrails. The staircase was complemented by a red and iron-colored vase sitting at the far corner of the living room where deer trophies were mounted on the high walls. Again, Mr. Walsh had other plans in mind when he decided to decorate his living room with deer heads and foreign sculptures.

Not finding his father in his study, Nick jogged up the stairs leading to the narrow hallway with doors leading to each room on the floor. He went to one of the doors and tapped on it, pushing it open to find his father sitting up in his bed with two huge fluffy pillows supporting his back, and a book in his left hand. "Welcome home, son." He greeted with a smile as he dropped the book on the bed. Without a word,

Nick lowered himself on one of the chairs near the bed.

"Where is Adolph?" He asked without spotting his son's long and expressionless face.

"I left him outside. There is something I'd like to talk to you about."

Mr. Walsh removed his reading glasses and placed them on the side table.

"Dad, as I'm sitting right here with you, I think I may have lost the most important thing in my life." With Mr. Walsh's face blank and his eye-lids batting slowly, he rubbed his grayish beard saying, "I'm listening son." Nick turned his face away and continued, "Dad how could you? How could you have kept this away from me all these while?"

Mr. Walsh, out of patience for what Nick was about to say barked, "Don't test my patience boy. Say what's on your mind." He then stood on his feet and walked over to the liquor cabinet and brought out a short glass, pouring scotch into it. He then turned to his son and asked, "Lime?" Nick didn't answer him. He was rather angry and anxious to talk to his father, but Mr. Walsh wasn't a man to be rushed. He wasn't a man to be yelled at or scolded like a child either. He was an influential man and whatever his son had in mind had to wait till he had gulped his scotch.

As soon as he emptied the content of the glass into his mouth, he groaned as the hot drink traveled down his throat. "Dad you know you are not supposed to be drinking," Nick chipped in as he gaped at him. "Yes, but your advice came too late when the drink must have started doing more harm," he replied grimacing and let out a rough cough. "The doctor said I can drink just one short a day. So I guess this is the last for me." He said still laughing and returned to his bed and sat before his son.

"My dear, listen. I know whatever that is eating you up must be because of that girl. Matters of the heart require patience. Whatever it is she did, I'll talk to her. Okay?" Mr. Walsh said as he tried to sooth his son. "Dad, this is not about my relationship, I mean it's a part of it but not really what I've come to discuss. I've never been so humiliated in my life dad. I went to this foreign country because of love, only to be told that Grandpa Walter stole from their family years ago." Nick said as he stared at his father from the corner of his eye to catch his reaction. When there was no expression found, he continued.

He must have forgotten that his father wasn't a man to express his emotions so easily. He was best at quick calculations. Mr. Walsh adjusted himself on the bed, "So what has that got to do with us?" Nick, more infuriated, yelled, "It has everything to do with us dad! It has everything to do with me. I was threatened to leave the country or get harmed because of what Grandpa did. I mean do you even know the magnitude of what he did? The shame this has brought to our family and most importantly my intentions to marry Stella?" Nick screamed. "Now we are seen as the family of thieves. Her father didn't like me from the outset, let alone when he discovered the truth." Nick rambled on and didn't care to look at his father's face.

"Do you know anything about this, dad?" he queried.

"No I'm just hearing it for the first time. Although I

remember when your grandfather used to travel to Africa, but anyway, that is not necessary. If that's the bad luck then you can settle down with someone else here."

The response infuriated him even more so that he jumped to his feet inches away from his father, "What the hell are you talking about? You are sounding so insensitive right now. I thought you liked her?"

His father glared at him and sipped from the scotch glass he had offered Nick. "I did, until I realized she's useless…"

Nick was enraged. He was so close to strangling this old man whose lips only moved while his wrinkles and grey hairs made him appear more handsome for his age. *What a man!* "Now she's useless because there's no diamond to steal like grandpa did already? This is all you do! You only want to exploit people. You don't think anything good could come from a cordial relationship without you gaining something. I love that girl, diamond or not!"

By now, Mr. Walsh was back on his bed staring at the dark screen of the television in his room. All he was waiting for was for his son to finish lamenting and get out of his room. As expected, Nick realized that his father was no longer responding to him, so he left the room. Mr. Walsh watched the door slam, sending a puff of air to the cream flowered curtain at his window.

Days rolled into weeks as Stella anticipated a call from Nick. She wanted to hear him say there was a way out for the both of them to be together, to hear him speak to her in that soft and convincing voice he uses when he's sorry for his actions, but it hadn't happened, and, with the way things were looking, it wasn't likely to happen.

As she pranced around in the large compound with her cell phone in her pocket, her father appeared from the kitchen leading into the backyard. He noticed the worry written on her face but said nothing. He watched her from afar dialing a number and bringing the phone to her ear and then staring back at it with anger each time there was no response on the other end. He decided to make his presence known by walking closer to her gradually with his two arms folded behind him. The long white caftan he wore made him look taller than he was already. Stella frowned immediately when she saw him. She hadn't spoken to him in days, and there wasn't anything to be discussed now.

"Maybe he's busy, or just decided to leave you now that he knows you have a strong family." He began. "Taking advantage of people is what they do best and I'm not surprised if that is what he wanted to do; use you and dump you as he pleased. You already know how his grandfather stole from us. Believe me..." Chief Ndube continued but was cut short by Stella who yelled abusively at him. She wasn't interested in whatever he had to say or what anyone thought about the man she loves. All she wanted was just a phone call from Nick, and not her father repeating history.

"Don't ever yell at me like that again. You may have your feelings hurt but I am not your mate. I am only looking out for your interests here," her father responded. "Anyway, I came to remind you about the party my friend invited us to tomorrow. Your friend is now a surgeon and will be settling in Nigeria like any good son would." Chief Ndube prattled on without noticing his daughter's face. Stella, without a word, walked out on him.

She had suddenly remembered Obike her childhood friend. They grew up together while their fathers were best of friends. He was a charming and very intelligent man, and she knew that the dinner which they've been invited to wouldn't just be a welcome home gobble; it would lead to an impromptu engagement by the families.

She hadn't seen Obike in six years. They had written each other a few times after she traveled to Canada, but the communication blurred when she began dating Nick. In all his emails and phone calls, he always mentioned how much he wanted to spend the rest of his life with her. Now Nick is gone, Obike has returned, she will be dining with him in a close range, and what else, a marriage alliance?" she thought.

Shortly before dawn, Mathew returned from an errand and went into the living room to drop the car key on the tray. He whistled through the hallway and towards the kitchen. He noticed Paulina sitting in the backyard but turned his gaze towards the fridge. He opened it and bent down in search of something; it was the cold beverage he put in the fridge last night. Now he had returned to it thirsty and anxious to gulp it down, but it was missing. His face suddenly turned like a cloud. He went straight to the trash bin at the far corner of the fridge and peered through it and found the empty bottle of the beverage sucked dry and dumped like it never existed. Furious, he dashed out of the kitchen to where Paulina was sitting, frowning as he yelled her name continuously and spoke in pidgin, "Paulina! Paulina!! *Who drink my joose?*" his mouth shaped like a flute with the way he spat *joose.*

Paulina looked him up and down and sighed returning to what she was doing. *"You didn't hear me? Is it you that drink my joose?"*He queried her authoritatively without looking at her face. "What juice are you talking about?" Paulina answered him calmly but angrily. She knew how troublesome Mathew can be when he loses something. Most annoyingly, his English was a mockery.

"The joose I put in the fridge this morning. Who took it?" Mathew continued.

"Go to the fridge and look for it. Do you see me holding any juice here? Please Matty, leave me alone." Paulina retorted and rose to her feet.

"Leave you alone? *My joose is missing and you say leave you alone? Who else will drink it if not you? You are always drinking one thing or the other in this house. Is it a ghost that fly in to drink it?*" Mathew replied angrily and this time charging very closely at Paulina. The rate at which he blurted his grammar sent Paulina laughing out loud.

She continued to laugh that Mathew lost interest in the missing juice and began wondering what was so ridiculous about him that would make her laugh like that. He bent his head to stare at his feet up to his waist, and then returned his gaze to Paulina who was now smiling and shaking her head. "Maybe Stella drank your juice. You should ask her about it then." Paulina suggested and waited to hear his response. How was he to ask his boss's daughter if she drank his juice? This hilarious thought sent Paulina laughing again. When Mathew realized that his quest may have met a dead end, he slowly turned back into the kitchen quietly and disappeared into the hallway.

Chapter 7

The anticipated event to which Chief Ndube had invited his household was finally here. The event was to celebrate his old friend's son's return and also to build a stronger alliance with his friend who is into oil investment. As darkness embraced the bright clouds, Chief Ndube yelled for his wife and children to hurry up. He continuously glanced at his wrist watch and adjusted the white *agbada* he was wearing. and walked towards the mirror in the mini-bar to stare at his outfit. He gently positioned his round white cap properly and then looked up again, but this time he saw his wife coming down the stairs gently, gentle enough not to trip on the long pink, lace wrapper she tied about her waist. The dark-blue *gele*-scarf she tied on her head complemented the wild-gold chain and brown shoes she wore.

Soon Stella appeared from her room in a short-sleeved, knee-length sequined dress, the folds of which shimmered around her as she walked. It was a gift from Nick when he had returned from a diamond expo in Los Angeles. He had seen the dress in the display glass worn by a white mannequin that had the exact shape of Stella while driving on Rodeo Drive. Funny enough, he pulled over in front of the store and dashed in only to realize it was just a sample and the dress wouldn't be there till the next week. He had to pre-order it for the woman he loved knowing she would love it.

As Chike appeared from his room with a grey suit with light pink shirt and black flat shoe, he noticed his gorgeous sister frowning in a corner. He gently walked up to her and lifted her chin gently with his thumb and stared at her eyes. Her snapping, chestnut-colored eyes stared right back at him. He dropped his hand and moved towards the door. She didn't want to talk to anyone. To her, the whole event was a mockery, and to them, she was just unnecessarily emotional.

Chief Ndube, his wife and his son wordlessly followed Stella out the door. Chike and Stella rode in one car while their parents rode in another. It was a silent trip as the family finally pulled over before a white mansion, the parking crammed with automobiles and the lawn with guests giggling and chatting as they walked into the main house. A slow Oliver de Coque melody was heard from afar. Just like the day her father had thrown a welcome home party for her, and girls from all over town graced the occasion, so Stella saw lots of beautiful women her age at the occasion.

As Stella drew nearer into the large hall where the party was held, she picked up a glass flute filled with sparkling champagne and sipped it. She gently glanced around the room as if in search of something interesting to fix her eyes on. She glanced at her watch and brought out her cellphone from her clutch and checked to see if there were any missed calls from Nick. Disappointed at the blank screen, she threw the phone back into her purse, turned and asked the waiter to pour her more champagne.

With another glance, she saw her father shaking hands with his friends and laughing out loud. He continuously adjusted the agbada he was wearing. As

Stella tilted her head backwards to gulp the last drop in the glass, her brother appeared before her with a grin.

"The night is still young for that," he began as he dragged her through the crowded room to a different living room, close enough to be seen from the event hall. "Why are you punishing yourself? You are here to have fun. For God's sake, act like it. Look around you, everyone is enjoying themselves. Go out there, engage yourself and make some friends," he scolded. His suggestions were falling on deaf ears. She was now tipsy. Chike could sing all night if he wanted; she wouldn't listen. She hadn't forgotten that he had joined her father to send Nick away, so what would he care about how she decides to enjoy herself at the party?

"I didn't want to come -- you and dad made me, so this is my own idea of having fun." Stella retorted. "Okay, so now you are here, why don't you just relax? Obike has been looking for you." Chike replied, hoping that his last comment would cheer his sister up.

"Well, I'm not looking for him." Stella replied drunkenly. Immediately, they were interrupted by a tall light-skinned man with dark, rich, spotted waved-hair, wearing a lavender shirt and black pants. With his right hand in his pocket and the other holding a wine glass, he walked over to Stella with a smile. Stella recognized him. How could she forget those sparkling white teeth, his naturally trimmed brows and pink-red lips that always looked like they were begging for a kiss? How could she forget how handsome he always looked? Out of touch, she squealed and hugged Obike. Chike, hoping that he was leaving his sister in good hands instead of with glasses of champagne, disappeared into the crowd. "Look at you, Mr. GQ, ever stylish!" Stella teased as she stared at his wide chest.

"Wow! I'm speechless. I've been looking for you. Your dad told me you'd come. Thank you for showing up, *ma*," Obike spoke softly.

This was another quality he possessed that women went crazy for; he was slow to speak and a good listener. "Don't mention it. Congratulations on your degree, and welcome home." Stella continued, this time her eyes fixed on his lips as they moved.

"Honestly Stella, I can't believe you stopped replying my messages. What did I ever do to you? I called and left messages with no reply." Obike complained.

Stella felt guilty at hearing him but tried to defend herself. "I know, I got busier, and I met someone," she confessed with a guilty smile, hoping to throw him off. She knew that was the last thing Obike expected to hear from her knowing how much he professed his feelings through his emails.

The music changed from one traditional song to the other. Soon women gathered at the center stage to dance. Stella was quickly distracted by this but regained her focus toward the man with whom she was speaking.

"Still, you should have told me. We've been friends for God knows how long and my feelings wouldn't have changed even if you got married," Obike replied, looking intently at her face. There was a certain sparkle in those eyes that made Stella feel pity for him. She wasn't in love with Obike, and there was absolutely nothing to feel guilty about.

"I know. It's my mistake. I should have called," Stella explained, "…and replied to the emails," Obike joined with a smile as he continued to stare at her. She averted her eyes.

"Yes, replied to my emails, and…", Obike moved closer to her, so close that she could not only smell the cologne he was wearing but his minty breath as well. The glasses of champagne she gulped down earlier were beginning to affect her even more now, breaking down her defenses.

The DJ must have gotten a tip that someone needed to be held, so he quickly switched the traditional music that was blaring all along with Shania Twain's "From a Distance." Obike gently bent towards Stella's ear, pecked her cheek, then whispered, "May I have this dance?" Stella who was still absorbing his proximity didn't know what to answer. She just smiled and waited for him to make the move by gently taking her hand. He wrapped his thick arms around her curvy waist bringing her so close to him that her breasts brushed his thick, wide chest each time she moved in the rhythm of the song. For a few minutes, all thoughts of Nick disappeared. She must have forgotten how long she had been leaning on Obike as they gently swayed to the music. As she turned to look over her shoulder, she noticed her father and her brother beaming a smile at them. Breaking the weak spell, she regained herself and quickly pulled away from him and ran out of the room with her dress floating with the wind. She stopped at the parking lot and began searching for her brother's car. Frustrated, she fished out her cell phone and began dialing his number.

Spotting Obike running towards her from afar, she began walking faster. All of a sudden, she missed her step and twisted her ankle and shrieked as she gently lowered herself to the floor of the parking lot. Obike rushed to her with pity written all over his face. He bent to examine the injured leg. Again, she felt his warm and soft palm on her slim ankle. She gently closed her eyes and moved strands of hairs on her face to the back of her hair and pretending not to notice his sexy body.

"And what is it are you are running away from now, Stella?" Obike asked as he was examining the leg and applying slight pressure at the joint to feel the swelling. Stella groaned in pain to avoid answering the absurd question.

"Did I do something wrong?" he asked, this time looking at her and then returned to the leg. "You will be fine. Just don't move around. I'll call my driver to take you home. Better still, let me come and help you to your room." He continued. Stella wondered if he was asking her or suggesting an idea to her.

At this time, she didn't have any better answer, so she nodded like a child. Soon she saw Chike her brother walking towards the parking lot with his phone in his hand. He seemed to be searching for her. As soon as he saw his sister on the floor, he ran to her with a frown. After being briefed about her state, Chike decided to take his sister home. Obike still concerned about her state, promised to visit her tomorrow.

As Stella and her brother drove home without a word to each other, she kept glancing at Chike's lips to see if he would ask her what had happened. Chike was slow to speak most of the time, preferring to think more. Sometimes, people teased him because of his silent attitude, but that night, Stella wanted her brother to speak, to speak his mind no matter how hurtful it may sound. Out of patience, she broke the silence, "I miss him…" Still nothing came out of Chike's mouth; rather he seemed to place all his concentration on the road. He wondered if it was his sister that was talking at that moment or the alcohol influencing her.

"Chi, you lived with him; you were very close to him. Tell me what he could be thinking." she pleaded tearfully as she sought closure from her brother. She stared at her brother's lips again to see if they will move this time.

"Have you called him?" He asked, summoning courage to satisfy her sister. "Millions of times but he's not answering. I don't know what to do." She replied. "What is it about this boy that has rubbed you off your sanity? Don't you see the fine print? He doesn't want you anymore. That's why he hasn't called nor returned your calls. What more proof do you need? If you go to Canada, what is the probability that he will still want you?" Chike lashed out at her as he held tightly to the steering, peering through the rear view mirror for oncoming cars.

"He loves me! You all drove him away, that's why he's not responding." Stella defended quickly. She knew how irrational Chike could be, and it was only sensible that she corrected him immediately. She stared at the road as her brother drove without further words.

Chapter 8

As Nick sat down in the leather couch in his living room, he picked up the black remote which was lying beside him and began searching for something to watch on the TV. He pushed the buttons continuously as his mind wandered to Stella. He hadn't spoken to her since he arrived and it had been a week already. What could she be up to, and what would be his excuse for not contacting her since he returned to Canada? He contemplated, thinking it would be easy to forget everything about Stella instantly being that he could have any woman he wanted, but as the days drew longer, he realized he couldn't stop thinking about her.

"Simple task, simple instruction," Mr. Walsh barked at his son, "You couldn't accomplish! How am I even supposed to entrust the entire company into your hands if you can't even make small sacrifices?" Nick ignored his father's rave and kept browsing through a large portfolio on his office desk. He tapped his fingers on the desk gently absorbing everything his father would throw at him. "Your grandfather who left this legacy for us didn't just hand it over to me because I was his only son, he trusted my judgment and was pleased with my efforts," Mr. Walsh continued as he rubbed his thin grey hair backwards.

"And what you want me to do is to steal from the woman I love? Is that what you call sacrifice?" Nick retorted. "That's what sons do to impress their father?" Nick snapped shut. As soon as Mr. Walsh realized his son was no longer responding to him, he quickly got up and let the office.

When Nick saw that he had left, he relaxed his back on the chair and adjusted his striped-sky blue tie which coordinated with the white shirt he was wearing. His mind reeled on what his father had just said. He was in a dilemma, yes a dilemma of ignoring his father and being with the woman he loves, or pretending to love Stella while his eyes are on her family's wealth again.

He was quickly interrupted by his phone which chimed in an increasing tempo. He turned around and peered into the screen. On seeing Stella's number, he hesitated for a few seconds and then picked up the phone. As soon as he heard her voice say, "hello," he felt a rush down his arms and gently blinked his eyes. "Sweetest, are you there?" She spoke. He drew a long breath and finally spoke into the phone. "Yes I am, Baby. How are you?" He waited for her reply as he began tapping his ball pen on the desk, distracted by the inscription on it. "Why are you punishing me like this? Why have you decided to ignore me?" her voice echoed through the line.

In search of an answer, he continued to tap the pen on the table. He knew he was wrong not to have communicated with her, but something else was bothering him. In as much as he wanted to be with her, he still couldn't bring himself to lead her on. He stands to lose a multimillion dollar company if he didn't do as his father said. "I have to go now baby. I have a meeting in a few, I'll call you later." He replied and hung up the phone without waiting for her response. The truth was that he had no answer for her questions.

Stella stared at the phone for a few minutes, her mind filled with thoughts and worry. Nick had never hung up the phone on her, not even if he was headed for a meeting. He was the son of the CEO, so whatever meeting he was attending would wait for him; he didn't have to rush to it. She realized he had lied to her and there was nothing she could do about it. In other to confirm her worries, she redialed the number and placed it in her ear as her eyes rolled around slowly anticipating his voice but unfortunately, the call went to voicemail. She dropped the phone and slumped on her bed and pounded her pillow angrily, screaming into it. Her tears and makeup stained the pillow.

She didn't hear the knock on the door until Mathew walked in. He didn't wait for her to ask him why he was there as he said, "Madam, your friend don come — your friend is here to see you." She ignored Mathew and continued to hide her face in the pillow. "Get out! I do not wish to see anyone right now," she ordered. Mathew shivered in fear and rushed out of her room with a frown.

Few minutes later, Obike entered the room gently as he tapped on the door. "Stella, is everything okay?" He asked gently hoping she wouldn't hurl anything at him.

"Go away..." she yelled.

"I've come to take a look at your ankle. How are you feeling today?" He asked as he drew closer to her bed where she was lying with her face buried in the pillow. "I am fine, please go away." She muttered through the pillow. "Then let me see for myself."

Obike insisted now sitting on her bed. He gently placed his soft palm on her shoulder and squeezed it. "C'mon, baby, look at me. I'm sure whatever it is can be discussed over few scoops of ice-cream." Stella gently wiggled her body away from his touch and stood up, exposing swollen pink eyes from crying. She looked at Obike and then looked at her sheets. "I am sad, and I don't want to be treated to ice-cream like a child," she gently responded.

"I've known you since you were eight, and if there's anyone worth sharing this pain of yours with, it's me. You can talk to me like we used to before. Come..." He pressed and stretched his arms to hug her. She gently fell into his arms and sobbed on his grey jacket. He frowned at her sorrow and squeezed her back gently. "It's okay to cry. Whatever it is that is hurting you will soon pass away. I promise you that." On hearing those words, she sobbed more and hugged his neck tightly. He dipped his right arm into his trouser pocket and brought out a handkerchief and began dabbing the tears on her face gently. She collected the piece of cloth and wiped her face further. Drawing a long breath, she stretched forth her leg for him to examine. He continued to stare at her face while she stared at her leg, because there was nothing else to stare at. Finally Obike bent his face to exam the injured leg. He tried to wiggle the foot but she flinched. "No more pressure on it for a couple of days. No dislocation...small swelling....probably a sprain...but you'll be fine. Place ice on it every few minutes to ease the swelling." He concluded "If you continue to cry, it may take forever to heal." He added with a smile on his face.

This made Stella smile for the first time that day. "You haven't changed with your jokes, you know?" she teased.

"I haven't. You can say that again." She caught his expression and tried to change the topic. "I am still the Obike you used to know; especially the one who loves you more," he dropped. Stella felt uneasy as soon she heard those words. She liked Obike as a friend, and this was simply too much for her to bear in one day. All she wanted was answers, as to why Nick was suddenly acting so strangely towards her.

It was a Friday evening when Nick and his two other friends gathered around a small high table at Dave and Busters sipping a beer and chatting. Nick stared at the flat screen TV mounted across the room. There had been a plane crash in Virginia, but the noise in the large room made it impossible for him to hear the details. He then returned his face to his friends who had been discussing last night's game. Zack, who couldn't help but notice his friend's moody state, turned to Nick asking, "What's the matter buddy? You've been just staring at your drink." Nick realized how his mood was affecting everyone in the table. He wished they hadn't invited him, but at this stage he needed to consult his friends for advice. Corry and Mark turned towards Nick, anticipating a response. Zack lifted the beer bottle and gulped down the contents as he observed Nick. "It's surprising that our rich boy is sad. C'mon talk to us," he scuffed. Nick shook his head at Zack's response. "Ok, I think I lost. I hate to lose..." He began. "What did you lose? Did you gamble? I thought you got all the money, mate?" Zack teased again laughing loudly this time.

Mark hurled the beer top at him playfully. "I'm serious guys. I just lost my girl." Nick continued. "Which of them?" Cory asked and again Zack and Mark busted into laughter. The noise increased at the table as the men entertained one another.

"How many of them do I have? Guys, be serious! I'm talking about Stella," he yelled with a slight anger on his face. There was silence among his friends as they sipped their beers.

"What happened?" Mark asked with seriousness on his face. "The first lady, huh?" Cory chipped in.

"I don't know. We are falling apart." Nick replied innocently. "Didn't you follow her to Africa? I thought you two were together there?" Zack asked.

"Yeah I did but things went wrong. Her father is a racist and wants me nowhere near her." Nick answered.

"Oh, wow!" Mark exclaimed.

"Yeah mate, that's terrible. Where is she?" Zack asked.

"Still in Nigeria," Nick replied.

"That's messed up, bro. So what's the deal? Do you two still talk?" Cory asked. He was the least to speak among them.

"I don't know. I haven't spoken to her. I don't know what to say guys. My dad is on my neck. Apparently he learned her family deals in stones too and now he wants me to get some from her. The problem is that I don't want her to feel like I'm with her because of her family's business,"

"They deal in stones too? Man I heard the stones from Africa are really good shit. They fetch you lots of dough you know? Your dad is a wise guy " Zack prattled on, ignoring the main issue.

The three men glared at Zack forwardly and he regained his sense. "Yeah what I meant was, why would your father ask you to do that knowing how you feel about her?" Zack asked seriously.

"This is so complicated. You know what I think? I think you should just level with her. If she's gonna be with you then she will be." Cory reasoned.

"What are you saying, buddy? Tell her that he wants to steal from her family while still being in love with her?" Mark argued.

"I didn't hear him say steal." Cory defended.

"Then what is it? Obviously her father sniffed the thief from afar," Zack joked again.

"Okay guys. I don't want her family's wealth. I love her. I just don't know what to do. Her father hates my color, and he says it out loud. You should have seen the way he looked at me the first time we met. How am I to convince him to allow me to marry her?" Nick said, "and I stand to lose my company as well, if I flout my father."

"That sounds like a suicide mission, mate." Mark replied, shaking his head in disapproval. The two men spent the rest of the evening arguing and discussing of better ways to solve Nick's problems. Nick got home hours later, drunk and tired. He entered his room and slumped on the bed. Thoughts of Stella kept rushing through his mind and all of a sudden he began feeling guilty and blaming her at the same time. He mumbled to himself a couple of times as he stood up to undress. He was so tipsy that he could barely keep his eyelids open. He slipped his hand into his trouser pocket and brought out a complimentary card which was given to him by one of his customers who works as an escort.

He brought the card closer to his face to read the name on the card as if he was seeing it for the first time. He then brought out his cell phone from the other pocket and began dialing the number on the card. He waited for a response. A soft voice echoed into his ears saying, "Hello Sugar," He rolled his eyes, rubbing his face gently. "I want to speak to Stella," he replied. "Sweetie, it's me, Amber. I was in your office today. I was wondering when you were gonna call me," the voice replied. "I want Stella, my Stella. Put her on the line please."

He continued in his drunken state, ignoring the voice. "Alright, baby. I'll be your Stella for tonight. Where are you?" the voice asked. "I'm home. Come to me, I miss you. I'm at 15 Bloor Street, in Rosedale." He spilt out without a second thought. "I'll be there honey," the voice sang and hung up. He continued to mutter Stella's name as his phone slipped off his palm.

The bright sunlight shone directly on Nick's face the next morning, and as he turned to hide his face, he noticed a tall, slender brunette in his bed. His eyes were still so weak that he rubbed them vigorously to see clearly. He sat up, peeped through the blanket and discovered that they were naked. Still confused, he stared at the woman further till she opened her eyes. She gave a weak smile and drew closer to cuddle him but he pushed her away angrily.

"How did you get in here?" he shouted. The lady gently got up and picked up her panties and slipped into them. She found her bra and short skirt together at the far end of the room. Without a word, she began dressing.

Nick watched her every move. He didn't remember bringing a woman home last night, but she was beautiful. That was a consolation for him.

"I knew this would happen. Can I have my money, please?" She said with her face expressionless.

"What happened? I'm sorry I'm confused here. What's your name again?" Nick asked.

"My real name or the one you gave me last night?" she retorted sarcastically.

"Anyway what does it matter...Did my friends send you here?" He continued to ask without an atom of memory of his escapades last night. He had forgotten everything; how he ripped her clothes off her roughly; how he called her Stella numerous times, and how he rammed her all night.

"My fee is two-hundred bucks, but for the extra stuff you made me do last night, I'm doubling it," she said.

Without a word, Nick glanced around for his trousers, a bit hesitant to stand up knowing he was naked. He dragged along the comforter to hide his nakedness and then picked up his trousers. He dipped his hand in the puffy side and brought out a wallet. He counted out a few hundred dollar bills and threw them to her.

She wordlessly picked up the money, counted it and smiled. "Thanks for your generosity. I guess my performance was worth more than two-hundred bucks." She grabbed her small bag and walked away. "Call me if you need me again tonight." She yelled and winked from the corridor.

Nick was filled with disgust as to how he had descended to sleep with a prostitute. He pounded the desk beside him a few times and rubbed his head. A tear escaped his right eye. He checked his watch lying on the table for the time and ran into shower. There, he stayed scrubbing his body, hoping to wash away last night's event.

Chapter 9

Mathew had always admired Paulina especially from behind when she bent to do her chores. Sometimes he would stand from afar, staring and moaning at the sight of her large buttocks. He hadn't summoned up courage to approach her until that cool evening when Paulina was squeezing her laundry in a bucket with her waist bent backwards facing where Mathew was standing. Unawares, he crept up to her and gently tickled her hips. She flinched and swept a harsh slap across his face. "What nonsense is this, Mathew?" She barked, calling him Mathew instead of the petty Matty she normally called him.

"What is the meaning of what?" Mathew retorted, rubbing the slapped cheek gently with a frown. "I've warned you severally not to do that again. I am a married woman and won't condone such…"

Mathew knew all that details because she always repeated herself each time he made advances at her, but when she would finally give up, was a mystery to him.

"You are a widow and that's why I don come to take care of business. Look at me na, look at fine boy like me you are rejecting. — Don't you see how handsome I am as you reject me?" he demonstrated with pride as he pressed his shirt to show off his rather plump looks. "I have money, dollars," he prattled on and brought out the money Nick gave him at the airport. He purposefully didn't exchange it because he needed to show off the foreign currency. Most importantly, to

the woman he admired.

Paulina's eyes widened at the sight of the dollars. She wondered if he stole the money.

"Mathew, Mathew, I've warned you, leave me alone!" She bent to continue what she was doing. Mathew at seeing the sight again whistled out loud. "*Choi!*" He exclaimed with his hands on his head. He was at the verge of going to touch her again when Obike entered the compound. Mathew quickly turned to him with a smile and his two hands folded behind him obediently. "Welcome, sir," he greeted cheerfully. Paulina smiled at him and greeted as well as if nothing had happened. He waved at them and walked into the living room. He had been to that house as many times and still remembered Paulina as the lady that always gave him biscuits when he was there to see Stella in their younger days.

When Obike came into the room, Stella was lying on the couch as she browsed through the City People magazine with its weddings and fashions. She quickly sat up and went to hug him as if he was the only face she expected to see that evening. He held her tightly and pecked her left cheek. They both disengaged and went to sit down. "My ankle is fine now, see?" She prostrated her healed leg for him to see.

"I can see with the way you jumped on me," he teased.

"I didn't jump on you," she argued shyly.

"Yes you did, "Obike debated. "I'm not here about your ankle; I'm here to see you." Stella looked at his face, that face that always melted her defenses and the puppy eyes that always spoke for him.

"I thought about you all day yesterday, most especially the sadness on your face. I'm glad you are smiling today and that I'm part of the reason why." He said softly. Stella didn't know what to say to him but smiled. "Why don't we take a drive to somewhere nice and leave this house for once?" he asked.

Without hesitation, she got up and took her magazine with her saying, "I'll change into something comfortable. Give me a few minutes." She smiled and walked away. Obike nodded back and relaxed on the sofa, waiting.

A few minutes later, Stella emerged, clad in a floating, blue knee-length dress, black flat shoes with her hair pulled back in a loose pony tail. She dressed simply and to the occasion. Obike turned and stared at the beautiful sight approaching him. At that moment, it struck him that he must do everything possible to have her and nothing would stop him. He led her into his car and drove off.

They arrived at Gordon's restaurant in Victoria Island, situated at the sea shore. The waitress cheerfully led them to the table where they could see the stunning city skyline. Obike walked around and pulled the chair for her to sit. She smiled as she stared at the beautiful vista in the distance. The evening was creeping in and the city lights came on, decorating the sky scrapers at Lagos Marina while the wind serenaded the ocean.

The waitress handed them the menus and brought out a note pad and pen from her apron. She waited for them to browse through the folder and place their orders. "Amongst these exotic drinks, which would you recommend?" Stella asked the waitress, smiling.

This was her first time to dine out of her home since she had returned from Canada. The waitress peeped at the menu and explained, "I'd recommend the bloody Mary, if you enjoy something with more than a hint of alcohol in it, otherwise the Caribbean coconut is my favorite."

She caught Stella's interested face and continued, "Would you like to try that?" Stella nodded in approval. The waitress turned to Obike, "and you sir, would you like the same?"

Obike replied, "Yes, I'll have whatever my lady is having," winking at Stella.

The waitress disappeared from the table and into the kitchen. Shortly, she appeared with two tall glasses filled with a creamy liquid with a small umbrella attached to them. Stella didn't look at the drink but stole glances at Obike when he wasn't looking. She admired his fashion sense; the light purple shirt he wore exposed the sparse but inviting hair on his chest. Maybe he left the first and second button open on purpose, she thought, or maybe he just likes to wear it like that. His dark rich hair which formed a sexy spotting wave gave him a neat and classy look. Obike was one of the people created on a Sunday, the day that God chose to take his time for better creations.

"Mmmm…this is good," Stella exclaimed as she sipped her drink. A certain spark appeared on her face. She rejoiced like a kid and kicked Obike under the table. It was this child-like behavior that Obike adored. He just watched her giggle.

"So tell me, who was this man that beat me in the game?" Obike asked. "There wasn't any competition at first, Obi," she replied, trying not to answer the question fully.

"So where is he? What does he do? What makes him so special?" Obike asked curiously. He wanted to know why his childhood friend fell in love with this ghost man.

"His name is Nick and he's a jeweler. He manages his father's company in Toronto and he's white." She blurted with a shy look.

"Get out of here!" Obike teased playfully. "He's white? How come?" he inquired, getting more interested in her friend's life.

"Yes he is, and gorgeous too." Stella fed his curiosity.

"You said a jewelry company in Toronto? Was that where you did your internship?" Obike asked further as he sipped his drink.

"Yes! That's where we met," she replied.

"Why did you run away from me that night at the party? Was it because of him? Where is he now?" Obike found himself pouring out a million and one questions to her. He wanted to know every detail.

"He came back with me, but Dad didn't like him. There were other issues, too, so he left. We haven't talked much. The last time I called him, he rushed me off the phone. I'm guessing he doesn't want to talk to me."

Stella found herself pouring out her heart to Obike. She had forgotten that he too admired her. "I'm sorry to bore you with my sad story. Anyway, right now I'm just here. I will go back to work for Dad's company on Monday." She finished when she realized she was giving away too many information to Obike.

"No you are not boring me, but if you insist…" he said, hoping she'd stop talking about him. He has heard enough to make his heart beat in jealousy. After they finished their drinks, he paid the waitress and they drove off. They arrived at a park in Ikoyi as darkness crept in on them. He led her through a lighted wooden bridge that crossed over to the main park. This was a place lovers come to lounge together in the evening.

As they sat on a metal bench, he took her hand and placed his wide soft palm on hers. Bringing her hand closer to his cheek, he peered into her eyes saying, "I do not want you to cry again like the way I saw you. I care about you so much." Stella's face was blank as she listened.

"I don't know what this man did to you but I do know that any man who would hurt his woman doesn't deserve her."

Obike's words touched her heart and she began to see him in a different light.

"I think he needs time to think things through. Who knows…" she began but was interrupted by Obike who pulled her closer and kissed her. She lost her breath and melted. His lips were thin and wet as they gently sucked on Stella's lower lip. They disengaged and Stella pulled away from his grip. "Obi, we've known each other since we were children and I never cast a lustful eye on you. This fire you are igniting is dangerous, so dangerous that it may burn us both." Stella said.

"All my life I've known you and watched you rejoiced and cried. Throughout your stay in Canada, the thought of you never left my mind. I want to tell many things; I want to tell you how I truly feel, but with this hurt in your heart for another, how do I speak without appearing flippant?" Obike replied, but this time his charm didn't give the speech.

"This is heavy for me, Obi," she confessed.

"I know that, Baby, but look back and see how much we've grown, and how far we've come," he continued. "This fire will only continue to burn," he concluded.

"It's getting chilly out here. Let's go," she said as she stood up and walked back to his car. Obike followed her without a word. She slumped into the passenger seat and waited for him to drive her home. Two months passed without Stella hearing from Nick. She was sure he had moved on with his life without a second thought.

Truthfully, he had thrown himself back into his work, and hadn't really thought about what she might be doing in his absence. He was confident that, someday, Stella would walk through his office door, confessing how much she loved him and wouldn't mind disobeying her father to be with him.

He decided to call her and wish her a happy birthday, so he had picked up his cell phone and began dialing her number. He listened for a response but all he heard was the normal MTN automated response: *the number you've dialed is not available at the moment, please try again later.* His heart palpitated in frustration as he redialed the number but met the same message. He wondered why her number wasn't going through but told himself it was simply network inconsistencies.

While Nick wondered why Stella hadn't returned his calls if she saw his missed calls, or why the network was misbehaving, Stella was having the time of her life with Obike.

After few dates with Obike, she began to see how much he loved her. Their friendship was no longer the young friendship that ended in the library, or at home watching TV. They were grown adults now and whatever they liked in each other while younger was now stronger now they were adults. But Stella had to admit that Nick was still her true love. She missed him so much but had to stick to her guns by not contacting him either since he decided not to call her. She always felt that someday, Nick would walk through the door, holding roses, and getting on his knees to ask for her forgiveness. But what is there to forgive, for abandoning her because her parents rejected him, or for her not being able to stop her father from chasing him away? She pondered.

Chief Ndube was in the garden reading newspaper while his wife knitted wool when Obike entered with pink roses in his hand and a wrapped package on the other. He greeted the couple cheerfully. Chief Ndube peered at Obike through his reading glasses and returned his gaze to the newspaper he was holding. He waited for him to turn to the main door before nudging his wife. "You see what I'm saying?" He whispered.

"Which is?" she replied, unconcernedly.

"I think she's finally coming around. I'm glad she's gotten over that thief."

Martha gave her husband a long look and continued knitting. At last she said, "You think it's easy to separate two people in love? Why do you keep calling him a thief? It was his grandfather that stole from your father, not him." Chief Ndube knew that an argument with his wife was pointless because she refused to see things from his side. "A family of thieves gives birth to thieves. Obike is a better man for our daughter; he's a surgeon, has good looks, and from a good family. What else can a father ask for in a suitor?" he argued.

Martha drew a long breath and sighed. "You are the master planner of everything. Just keep in mind that it is her happiness that matters. I like Obike and I see them together as a couple but, truth be told, she loves Nick more."

Chief Ndube couldn't wait for her to finish before interrupting her, "eh-hen, what is the matter then?"

Martha paused, absorbing her husband's interruption, and continued. "All I'm saying is that just because they look good together doesn't mean they will remain happy. She chose a man for herself, and I think it's only fair we allow them to be."

Chief Ndube on hearing the last few words from his wife sighed and turned to his newspaper. He shook his feet agitatedly, and a frown crowned his face all of a sudden. Martha on the other hand smiled gently to herself knowing that her husband wasn't happy about her remark, but at the same time she enjoyed it when she gave him a reason to keep quiet about matters of the heart.

Obike had proven how much he loved Stella by spending every little time he had off from the OR with her. He knew that if he continued to push his luck, Stella would finally surrender herself to him, but when it would happen, he knew not. As he left work that Friday evening, he drove to Stella's office and hurried her to his car as if there was something to be missed in the next hour. Stella, confused, queried him as he drove her. He kept glancing at his watch as he sped through the highway and into the park. He kept smiling all through and stopped near the trees. Stella couldn't help but smile at his hastiness. She wondered what had finally come over him.

He got out the car and ran to her side and opened the door. Stumbling through the sandy path, she followed him to the hill surrounded by large trees where there was a stream flowing south. He glanced at his watch for the last time and quickly went behind her and covered her eyes with his sweaty palms. Now this madness ceased to be funny anymore, and Stella wondered what was going on.

"Shsss…wait…wait…almost…" he whispered in her ears.

As the sunlight appeared from its hiding place behind the mountains, Obike was beguiled at the beautiful site of the golden circle that was passing by before darkness crept in. He gently removed his palms from Stella's eyes so she could see for herself what he had seen. Stella's mouth was wide open as she too witnessed the beauty. She stretched her right hand as if she could touch the sun which looked like it was just inches from her reach.

Laughter escaped her lips as Obike stood in a corner watching her as she admired the breathtaking evening light. The fading sunlight on her skin made her lighter in complexion and smoother. Her white teeth shone as she smiled. Noticing Obike's eyes on her, she walked closer to him and said, "It's beautiful!

I've never seen anything like that before." Obike beamed at her and grabbed her waist, pulling her closer. He gently brought his lips closer to hers and kissed her. This time she wrapped her arms around his neck and kissed him deeply as well.

Obike turned her with her back facing him and gently kissed her neck. His cool lips sent immeasurable waves of sensation down her spine. She frowned and moaned in pleasure. He turned her sideways and kissed her cheeks and then back to her lips and breathed heavily in her ear. She turned around, hugging him tightly and, this time, clenching his shoulder.

Staring deeply into her eyes, his hand lifted her pencil skirt and pushed her panties aside. He circled his index finger around her wet vulva. She fell weak to his neck and kissed it.

As his finger pushed upward into her, a soft moan escaped her lips. He moved his finger deeper and she clenched her legs together. Obike removed his shirt and dropped it on the ground exposing his smooth and fit torso and gently lowered her to the grassy floor. Darkness had become their shield in the lonely park as he ripped her shirt and bra away and covering her nipples with his lips. He quickly unbuckled his belt and pulled down his briefs and pushed himself toward her. He stopped and continued to suck on her nipples while Stella moaned, begging him to make love to her. He wiggled his hips slowly and pulled her legs closer, pounding her ferociously while her nails dug deep into his flesh. When he was done, his head rested on her chest while she caressed it. Wiping the sweat from his forehead, he gently stroked her thighs. They lay there speechlessly, absorbing the fresh air that caressed their skin.

After numerous attempts to reach Stella without success, Nick's fears crept in on him. He found himself thinking of all possibilities of what could have happened to her or what she could be doing. He was in his office one afternoon when he received a call from *1-800-Flowers*. He had set up a plan for them to always deliver roses to Stella Every Friday when she was still in Canada, but since she was no longer in the country and their deliveries hadn't reached the recipient, they called to inform him. This made him realize how much he'd missed her. He found himself thinking about her more than he had imagined. He wanted to see her, by all means -- to watch her smile like she does when he looks at her; to see those deep dimples that form on her cheeks when she blushes. He picked up the intercom on his office desk and spoke to his secretary.

Chapter 10

Stella couldn't forget that memorable night that Obike proved his love to her. She lay in her bed as she picked her nails. The coating on her nails was peeling off and she wanted to help it further before going to the nail salon, but there were more pressing issues than the thoughts of Obike and her nails. As she found herself wondering between the two men in her life — who was more important, and who did she love more — Mathew, clad in faded khaki shorts and a blue t-shirt with a picture of a yellow rubber ducky on it, walked in with a tray in his hands. He smiled blissfully as he placed the tray of food on the table and waited to see if Stella needed anything else. Stella looked him up and down and then busted into laughter, saying, "Matty, wow! You are looking *extraordinary* today." Mathew looked down at himself and smiled back with gratitude. At the same time, he wondered what must have been making her so happy; she hadn't been this upbeat since her return from Canada.

"Thank you, madam," he replied. As he made his way towards the door, he asked, "Excuse me, madam, when is Oga Rick coming again?"
Stella lifted her brows and stared at him. She hadn't thought about it and wondered if that would ever happen. "You mean Nick?" she replied. "I don't know." She returned her eyes to her nails. She didn't see the dissatisfaction on Mathew's face as he left the room.
The family ties were getting stronger by the day, and

Chief felt it would be a good idea to invite Obike's parents for dinner. He had seen for himself how in love his daughter was with Obike, and the only reasonable solution was to tie the knot. He knew that a lot would be discussed during dinner, and if Stella agreed to marry Obike, then he would be looking at a bigger investment on his side; Obike's father would gladly invest in his company. It sounded like a well laid out plan at first, but it became a reality when the families gathered for dinner around the big mahogany table. As usual, the maids were at their best with their presentation as they served the guests. Stella sat beside Obike and listened as their parents conversed about politics, business, and then the matter at hand. Obike chuckled every once in a while at any funny remark that was made at the table. Suddenly he stood up with a glass in his hand; he picked up a fork and tapped it gently on the glass to gain the family's attention.

"Dad, mum, Chief, I'd like to make a toast to your honorable family and to the most beautiful woman in the world. She's my heartthrob and best friend." Everyone's face lit and Chief Ndube beamed and nodded at his daughter. Obike turned to Stella, who was blushing. He dipped his hand into his pocket and brought out a small black box. Martha's mouth opened at the sight of the black box.
"I know this may seem a bit awkward and a bigger surprise for my lady, but where else shall a man be proud to ask his woman's hand for marriage if not before her family?" Obike began as he glanced around the room. It sounded like a well prepared speech as everyone waited for him to finish. "I am

madly in love with this woman beside me," he continued, facing Stella. He adjusted his shirt, pulled the chair behind him backwards and went on his knees. He flipped open the black box, revealing the 10-carat diamond ring. With a smile and his sexy eyes begging the question, he asked, "Stella, will you marry me?"

Stella turned in astonishment. Her eyes caught his father encouraging her to say yes, and her mother begging her to ease the young man from the painful kneeling, and the maids all staring to hear her answer. She froze to her knees and her mouth searched for the words to say. She caught Matty's eyes in the corner with a frown on his face. Stella returned her eyes to the gentleman kneeling before her and stared at the ring. It was beautiful, and what woman at a marriageable age wouldn't die to adorn her finger with that? "Stella, I love you and want you. Don't you like the ring? Oh shit! I must have forgotten to ask you what type of stone you want on it. My mistake, I will have it fixed right now," he apologized embarrassingly and snapped his finger, beckoning his driver to appear before him. He handed the box to the middle aged man, saying, "Take this back and have them replace it with a…"

He stared at Stella, waiting for her to mention her choice of stone.

"Obike, please, you don't have to go through all that. I love the ring. It's beautiful and it's just perfect, but," she interrupted.

The family's faces gloomed in confusion and disappointment as they heard the last word 'but' escape her mouth. "But what, my love?" Obike begged for an answer and feared the worst.

"Sweetie, you've been great all through and nothing would make me happier than being your wife, but I just feel rushed. I don't think I am ready yet..."she retorted and quickly caught her father's eyes now about to shoot missiles her way.

Obike drew a long breath and wiped off the sweat from her face. "How long do you want me to wait? I've waited for years for this moment and prayed that you would be mine, and now you want me to wait again? Ok I'll wait. It's cool," he said angrily. Stella looked at him with pity, but she didn't want to tell a lie. She simply wasn't ready. With that, Obike quietly left and drove off with the company of his driver.

Chief Ndube, with the crush of disappointment written all over his face, raved at Stella, who seemed to be retracing her decision. Obviously she was now in a dilemma and her father wasn't making things easier for her. "What kind of response was that you gave out there?" Chief Ndube yelled at her as she sat on her bed. "What in the world is your problem? Don't we provide you with everything you want and need?" He continued despite Stella's unconcerned attitude. "You better call that young man and tell him something hopeful and positive, or else..."

"Or else what?" Stella retorted, now standing before her father. She was tired of his commands. "...Kill me or disown me?" She continued.

Chief Ndube stood before his daughter, mouth wide open, staring at her. Words couldn't escape his mouth. He was unable to finish his threats. "Try me child," he said and stormed out of her room.

Later that night, Obike returned to Stella's residence. He had something on his mind that he needed to clear. Stella was getting ready for bed when the gateman came to the door to announce Obike's presence. Surprised, she walked behind the gateman to see Obike's eyes glittering in the dark. She stood a few feet away from him in guilt. As he approached her, she bent her face downwards in search of what to say. "I am sorry I walked out on you," Obike said. Still Stella was speechless. "I went home to think things through, and I realized that I am the one who has failed to understand you. Therefore, it's okay with me and I am willing to wait till you are ready to marry me."

Stella lifted her face and stared and then moved her eyes down to the ground again. She hugged him tightly without a word as he gently squeezed her back. "You don't have to marry me as long as you are with me," he whispered.

"Do you still have the ring?" Stella finally asked with a teary voice as she wrapped her arms around him. Obike stepped back to make sure what he just heard came from her.

He looked into her teary eyes and asked, "Is that a yes?" Stella nodded with a weak smile. Obike squeezed his two trouser pockets in search of the ring but couldn't find it. He frowned as he looked further. He then brought out his phone and called his driver to find the ring and bring it to him. Impatiently, he pulled off his own gold ring from his middle finger and slipped it onto Stella's slender finger, hoping that she wouldn't change her mind before the real ring was found. Stella assessed the ring and smiled. She then kissed and hugged him. Obike found himself yelling into the night, "She said yes! She will marry me!" The gateman stood by the corner with the padlock in his hand, smiling at the two lovebirds. With that, Obike kissed her goodnight and rushed out of the gate as Stella stood there watching him.

In the wee hours of the morning, Stella was awoken by another harassing knock by Matty. This time it sounded louder than usual. With drowsy eyes, Stella opened the door and found Matty standing before her with a frown. "Madam, you have a delivery," he muttered.

"From who?"

"I don't know. Come and see for yourself."

Stella curiously slipped into her slippers and went to the compound and found a flower delivery van backing in. The driver appeared with a clipboard, asking her to sign a paper. She quickly signed the sheet and waited for the van to be unloaded. The driver carefully moved all sixteen vases of red roses into her bedroom. The vases were placed all over her bedroom. "Who sent them?" Stella asked the driver, who was about to get into the van. He brought out the clipboard again and scanned it and said, "It has no name, madam, but it says, from the one who loves you more."

This was becoming more interesting for Stella, who stood there wondering how romantic Obike could be to send her sixteen bouquets of roses that early in the morning. A smile appeared on her face when she thought about his witty ways of surprising her. She turned around and went to her room to smell the roses and then picked up her phone and dialed

Obike's number and awaited a response. As soon as his baritone voice slipped into her ear, she quickly began giggling and saying, "Wow Obi, you are so full of surprises. I don't know what to say this morning with all these roses in my rooms. I can hardly move around without bumping into them. They are beautiful!"

Obike knew he didn't send flowers to her but waited for her to finish before asking, "Which roses?" Stella's smile disappeared and a strand of seriousness crossed her face.

"Didn't you send me roses this morning?" Obike replied with a "No, I didn't. Does the recipient say my name on it?" Stella then realized she was excited for nothing. There were only two men in her life, and if Obike denied sending her the flowers then there was only one man who could have sent them. Her mind immediately reeled to Nick and what his agenda was by sending her the flowers. She quickly hung up the call with Obike and sat at the edge of her bed to think. She stared at her phone and began searching for Nick's cell phone number. Realizing that it was midnight in Canada, she decided to wait for a few more hours before calling him.

Martha knocked and walked into her room with a smile on her face, saying, "I heard the van drive off the compound and I came to see what was going on." She noticed the roses and added, "Those are beautiful. Are they from my in-law?" Stella shook her head and stared down. "Then who sent these beautiful flowers this early morning?" Martha queried, determined to find out who else would dot on her daughter.

"An admirer, mum…" Stella replied absent-mindedly.

Martha lifted one of the bouquets off the table and sniffed it gently saying, "Such an admirer must make himself known. I hope he's aware that you will be married in a month's time?" She gently placed the bouquet back to its place and continued, "By the way, I came to find out if you've decided where to go for your wedding shopping, and when?"

Stella lifted her face to stare at her mum and then returned her gaze to her phone as she continuously scrolled the track to every app. "I can't travel without my passport. Dad took it away before Nick left." Martha tapped her back saying, "Don't worry, I will get it for you. Is that to say that you've chosen Canada as your location?" Stella nodded without looking at her mother. "I shall go get it now," Martha said and walked out of the room.

As she watched her mother's back, a thought crossed her mind about going to Canada for her wedding shopping. In as much as she had decided to spend her life with Obike, she also wanted to see Nick once more. She still had feelings for him and thought it would be a good idea to see him so as to say goodbye that is if he no longer have feelings for her. Then another rebuking thought crossed her mind, "What if Obike goes with me on the shopping trip? How will I be able to be alone with Nick? What if Nick still loves me? I mean, telling from the roses, he still thinks about me." Suddenly, an idea came to her mind; something not even her father or Obike would suspect.

Chief Ndube was reading his morning news

when his wife entered the room and went to sit on the bed. He didn't turn to look at her but continued to read through the screen on the monitor. Martha broke the silence saying, "I spoke with her about the wedding and when she would like to begin shopping. She told me you still have her passport." Chief Ndube ignored his wife and continued reading. "So I think it would be best if you give it back to her," she continued, but was quickly interrupted by her husband.

"And how foolish do you think I am to allow her travel to Canada alone? Have you thought of why she wants to go to Canada to shop?"

"I guess she's familiar with it."

"Have you thought about who sent those roses to her?" Chief Ndube argued with his wife. He removed his reading glasses and stood up with his hands folded behind him. "I can only allow that trip if she will go with Obike. Let them do that shopping together!" he said with an air of finality.

Martha smiled, saying, "My husband is that why you are so worked up? Of course she will go with him. You need to trust her and let her be." She stood up and went to where he was standing and put her arms around his neck, saying, "Don't forget, if my father restricted me like you are doing now, we wouldn't have been married." He smiled, winked at her, and then stood up to peck her cheek and walked away.

As Nick lay on his bed, he couldn't help but think of why Stella hadn't tried contacting him to thank him for the flowers since the last time they spoke. He knew he owed her an apology, but a phone call to remind him that she still loved him was all he ever wanted. His instincts couldn't have lied about her father making sure she marries a proper Nigerian man instead of a foreigner like him. He was lost in thought when a call came in on his phone. He stared at it from the corner of his eye, not wanting to answer it.

As the ringtone increased its pitch, he was forced to check who it was. Recognizing his father's number boldly displayed on his touch screen phone, he frowned and answered the call. The last person he wanted to hear from was Mr. Walsh. Many conversations they had ended with Nick slamming the door behind him in anger or dropping the call. But these facts had not discouraged Mr. Walsh from his desires. He knew the only one who would help him fulfill them was none other than his son, Nick. "Dad," Nick bellowed on his cellphone and waited for his father to reply. "Dad I've already told you that I won't do it. I simply can't!" he yelled in reply and continued to listen. "Why don't you send Bruce, or better still, Adolph to fly down there and get them for you? Why can't you just leave me alone? You've already ruined everything." He barked and hung up the call in anger. At that moment, he decided he would travel to Nigeria, not to steal the diamonds as his father demanded, but to get back the love of his life.

Chapter 11

The airport was crowded with passengers checking-in their luggage and their loved ones standing around. Without a word from Obike, and Stella reading over the small print on her ticket, they waited for their departure. Stella lifted her chin to observe the crowd at the airport out of boredom. It seemed like she and Obike had run out of words to say to each other.

Obike gently squeezed her shoulder and snuggled her closer to his chest and planted a kiss on her forehead. He stroked her weave backwards as he joined her to observe the crowd as well. Soon, an announcement echoed, declaring their flight was boarding. Stella stood up with her bag and walked slowly in line with her fiancé as they entered the plane. They met a cheerful hostess who pointed them to their seats in the first class section. Shortly, the plane departed for Canada.

As the black 2004 Volkswagen cab pulled over in front of The Hazelton Hotel, Stella's smile returned to her face. She opened the door of the cab and stepped out. She stood at the side curb for few seconds to observe the city she had spent most of her adult life in. The cab driver stepped out of his car and went to unload their luggage. Obike paid him and waited for a hotel staff member to wheel their bags into the lobby. When Stella saw the restaurant across the hotel, memories clouded her head. It was one of Nick's favorite places to eat. They would go there every Friday with his friends and their girlfriends to eat and relax. Still lost in thought, she felt Obike's warm hand on hers. They both went into the elevator, which stopped on the fourth floor of the hotel. The hotel staff happily wheeled their bags into their suite. As the couple settled in, Obike noticed that his bride-to-be was absent minded, then he asked, "Does he know you are coming?"

Stella quickly looked at him in surprise and replied, "How do you mean?"

Obike chuckled and went close to the window to see the view. "Does your ex know you will be in Canada?"

Stella shook her head vehemently saying, "No. What made you ask?"

"You've been acting strange ever since we came here. Tell me again why you chose to shop in Canada, instead of other countries?" Obike queried.

"What are you driving at?"

"I don't know. It's a strange coincidence, don't you think?"

"I don't know what you want to hear from me, Obi, but it's been a long flight and I need rest," Stella retorted and walked into the bathroom to escape further interrogation.

It was a dull Saturday morning as Nick woke up and rubbed his eyes. He had gone out to drink with his friends the night before and slept immediately when he came home. Lonely, bored, and sluggish, he went to take a shower because he planned to go shopping before embarking on his trip to Nigeria. He wanted it to be a surprise to Stella and her family as well. After dressing up, he picked up the wallet he left on the dinning chair last night and shoved into the pocket without looking. He grabbed his car key, which he collected from his driver last night as he discharged his services. He wanted to drive himself and feel the city alone. With that, he took the elevator down to the car park and drove off in his Mercedes CLK.

After Stella and her fiancé had their breakfast in their room, she wordlessly went over to the dresser mirror and began applying her make-up. Obike, still noticing his fiancée's reaction, decided to set things straight.

"Did you really want me on this trip in the first place?" he asked. Stella ignored him and continued to paint her face.

"Even if you don't want me around, the least you can do is to look me in the eyes and answer my question!" he yelled as he moved closer to her.

"Do you really want the truth?" she retorted sharply.

"Yes, please tell me and save me from this game of yours."

"I am not playing games with you. I just feel like…" but she was interrupted by the telephone beside the bed.

Obike went to answer it and returned saying, "The taxi is here. We can deal with this later." With that, he grabbed his jacket and left the room. A few minutes later, Stella emerged from the room, clad in a bright blue dress and black sandals. She smiled at Obike who was reading a magazine in the lobby. They both entered the taxi and the driver sped off.

"So where do you plan to shop first?" Obike broke the silence again because he couldn't stand the lack of words between him and his best friend. It was unusual for the woman he loved so much to act like a complete stranger in another country. He had planned this trip to be like a pre-honeymoon for them, but her attitude was becoming unbearable. He just had to swallow it till they returned home.

"We have two weeks to stay in Canada, so I'm not rushing right now. I plan to simply visit some stores and return with their catalogues so I can carefully shop."

"OK…" Obike replied, unsatisfied with her response. Maybe she is nervous about the whole wedding thing, he thought to himself. He took her hand and kissed it saying, "It's alright. Let's just have fun with this shopping, okay? Meanwhile, I'd like to check out some stuff at Kenneth Cole and Joseph A. Bank today. I checked their online store and liked what I saw." Stella still didn't say a word. She fixated her eyes on the slow traffic.

Few minutes later, they arrived at the shopping plaza. Obike paid the cab driver and led his woman to the mall. They walked through Macy's store to the center of the plaza, which was surrounded by more outlets. Stella broke off Obike's grip and went to the directory board and began searching for a store. Obike met up with her and stared at the board in search of a store as well. They both went up with the escalator and Stella finally spoke to him, saying, "I'd like to check out some beads at Gerald's. I'll join you at JAB." Obike nodded and watched her disappear into the crowded plaza.

Finally she was alone and could breathe for a few without Obike either nibbling her ears or holding her hand like a dying woman. She wanted to shop on her own without his disturbance but since that was the only way she would be allowed to visit Canada one last time, she had to comply. Meanwhile, she still wanted an opportunity to thank Nick about the flowers, or better, see him one last time before her wedding. She had a lot to say to him and also wanted to find out why he didn't fight to make their relationship work. As far as she was concerned, her relationship with Obike wouldn't have happened without her father's pressure. Obike had been her childhood friend and love wasn't supposed to be involved, just a simple and honest friendship.

As Obike entered the JAB store, his eyes quickly caught a Hugo Boss light pink shirt across the room. He thought about how well it would fit him so he walked over to where the shirt was displayed. He lifted the sleeve to test for texture and then looked at the tag below it to find the material and price. Satisfied, he took a sealed pack of the same shirt beneath it. Turning around, his eyes caught a glass case that held wrist watches, necklaces and bracelets. He walked closer to observe the glittering watches. Momentarily, a voice interrupted him from behind, saying, "My girlfriend, or should I say my ex, bought the dark metal one over there for my birthday. It was a stud."

Obike turned his neck and saw Nick standing behind him with a smile and a shopping bag in his other hand. Nick gently rubbed his blonde hair backwards as he stared at Obike.

"I'm sorry; I shouldn't have loomed over you like that. I'm Nick, by the way."

Obike smiled back at him and brought out his right

hand for a handshake. "I'm Obi. Thanks for the recommendation. I was thinking of getting it as a gift to my father-in-law, but since you got it from your woman, I might as well keep it."

Nick chuckled saying, "I'd do the same if I were you. It's the best ever made by Bulova and you can at least boast of one."

"True. I came to shop for my wedding with my fiancée but she wandered into another store. Women..." Obike explained with a smile.

"I hear ya. Congratulations in advance. Well, I'm shopping for a trip as well. I plan to go and propose to my woman and see if she will marry me." The men laughed out loud.

"And if she refuses?" Obike inquired jokingly.

"Then I'll come back and drink myself to death," Nick replied, laughing.

"Where are you traveling to?" Obike asked.

"Nigeria," Nick replied happily. "Been there once and it was fun and unpleasant too. I gotta get going, but I'll return tomorrow to complete my shopping if I can."

"Interesting! I'm a Nigerian too. I live there as well. Maybe we can meet up for lunch sometime when you visit, or better still, you can come to my wedding," Obike replied.

"Absolutely! Why don't you write me your phone number and I'll give you a call as soon as I land in Lagos," Nick said. The two men exchanged phone numbers and Nick walked out of the mall, waving at Obike.

Stella walked from one store to the other, gathering catalogues and buying a few things. Exhausted, she went back to the center of the plaza and waited for Obike who was still in the store opposite, shopping. As she stared at his back, memories of Nick flooded her mind again. They used to come to the same plaza sometimes and leave hand in hand, eating Pinkberry Greek yoghurt and laughing at each other's jokes. As soon as Obike emerged from the store, she smiled weakly at him. They walked out the plaza and hailed a cab, which took them back to the hotel.

After the warm dinner that was served in their room, Obike broke the silence, saying, "I made a friend today at the store and invited him to our wedding." Stella didn't pay attention to what he was saying, but he continued, "He said he was traveling to Nigeria to meet a woman he loves, so I thought it would be nice to have him at our wedding." Still Stella kept mute. Obike stood up without noticing that she wasn't listening to him. "So what do you think?" he asked with a smile on his face as he stood before the bathroom.

Stella looked up at him and asked, "What do I think? You invited a complete stranger to our wedding and you are asking me what I think?" Obike was startled as the words lashed at him like a hide whip. "You should have thought about my feelings before inviting a complete stranger to our wedding." "Sweetie, it happened very quickly. We talked for a short time before I even brought up the wedding. What does it matter anyway? We have a guest list of 300 people attending this wedding from all over the world and 200 happen to be from your side, few of which I know, so what will one more head do?" Obike argued with a frown.

"It's not about the guest list! You just don't involve me in any of your decisions until you are done. To you it is just one head, but to me I see a stranger whom I don't even know hanging around. It's like having a wedding crasher!" She retorted angrily. As she argued, she knew it wasn't worth the energy, but she just had to vent her anger somehow.

As the couple argued, it dawned on them that the marriage might end before it even started. "Why are we arguing about this anyway? Why?" Obike asked calmly with his hands on his hip, revealing his toned biceps. "What is eating you up? You've been cranky ever since we arrived here." Stella ignored him and slumped on the bed with her eyes batting at the ceiling. Without further question, and seeing that she was not going to answer his questions, he went into the bathroom and bolted the door.

After a long, warm shower, Obike emerged from the bathroom with a towel tied round his waist, frowning. He stood at the edge of the bed and stared at Stella's back. She had already dozed off lying on her belly. Without a word, he picked up his deodorant and rubbed it gently on his armpits. He then removed the towel and slipped into his boxers and undershirt. Returning to the bathroom to hang the damp towel, he turned off the light and slipped into bed behind Stella. "I am sorry," he whispered in her ears and waited to see if she'd turn and face him, but she didn't. He began kissing her shoulder gently and caressing her hand but she wiggled quickly, pulling away from him. "I don't want us to fight no more. Can we get by this?" Obike whispered in her ears, but she kept moving away from his grip. He rested his case and pulled the blanket over his shoulder.

Chief Ndube was ready to leave for his office when he yelled for Mathew to bring his brief case. Mathew appeared with the brief case and waited for further instructions with his head bowed. Martha emerged from the kitchen with a smile as she went to kiss her husband. Chief Ndube not minding his wife's affection quickly asked, "Has she called?" Martha nodded. "Are they done with the shopping?" he asked.

"I spoke to her yesterday and she told me she was almost done with shopping, so we'll be expecting them in a few days," Martha answered obediently.

"I see. Mathew, you may go now," Chief Ndube said and Mathew disappeared in the corridor. He turned to his wife and led her to the living room. He stared at her for some time and asked, "Is everything alright in Canada?"

Martha nodded with a smile, saying, "I hope so. She didn't say if there was a problem or not. Is there anything wrong?"

Chief Ndube rubbed his beard and glanced at his watch. "I have to leave now. We will discuss further when I return." He leaned over to peck his wife and left the house. Martha watched from the window as his car rode off the large compound. She wondered to herself if everything was alright with Stella and Obike.

Chapter 12

The previous night, which was filled with resentment and frustration, introduced a quiet day with deep thoughts and emptiness. Obike and Stella were fully awake as they both lay in bed staring at the ceiling with a wide gap in-between them in the bed. They lay there for quite some time, wordless. Stella broke the silence, saying, "Do we have plans for today?"

Obike turned to her and replied, "I don't know. Do you?" She shook her head and remained silent. "How come you suddenly lack words to tell me? Is there something I'm doing wrong?" She didn't answer him. She alone knew that her aggression towards her future husband was unintentional but she couldn't hide how she felt about Nick.

"You can't even look me in the eyes no more. I am sorry if I did or said anything wrong. I can't take this silence of yours. We are supposed to be having fun shopping together and not fighting," Obike pleaded. This time, Stella turned and stared at his eyes and then picked on her fingers with thoughts running in her mind. "Do you still love me?" Obike asked, but she didn't reply. "Stella, do you still love me? Do you even want to get married?"

Stella looked at him and said, "I don't know." Obike was furious for the first time before her as he asked, "Then why are you here? Why did you even agree to marry me at first? I do everything to make you happy, but you treat me like I don't mean anything to you."

Stella glanced at him and said, "Obi, you know that's not true. I just feel weird about the whole thing. I'm stressed and I want everything to be right between us before we exchange vows. I care about you and want you and I to believe that is enough to be together." Obike couldn't contain his anger anymore as he barked, "What are you saying? Stella, are you high or something? Do you think I shouldn't be worried about if you love me or not? Do you think I want to marry you simply because you care about me? Some women have done that in the past and they proved it daily, but I realized they are not what I want. My heart belongs to you! There's no one else I'd rather wake up to but you! So tell me again what you mean when you say you don't know if you want to get married or not?"

Stella was now shaken by the way he was yelling at her. She sat up and held the fluffy pillow to her chest as tears gathered around her eyes.

"Is this your way of telling me you don't want to get married to me? Was that why...?" He stopped halfway and got out of bed. He pulled out his luggage and began ripping his clothes off the hanger and throwing them inside the bag.

Stella turned and stared at him packing angrily but said nothing. She turned her face away and snuggled the pillow closer. "I'm sorry Obi..." she muttered as tears rolled off her eyes.

"Mum, he's on his way back to Nigeria..." Stella spoke softly on the phone as she rubbed her hair. "I didn't say anything to him. I don't know, I guess this wedding probably came too soon, mum." She continued and stood up and went to the mirror.

She observed her cheeks and scratched on a small pimple that was coming out. "I don't know mum," she replied angrily to her mother. "We will talk about it when I come home. Please don't mention this to dad yet. I don't want him to panic."

She then supported the phone with her left shoulder as she pulled out her luggage and began checking what she had bought. "Yes mum, the wedding still holds." Her eyes caught a stain on the bottom of a pink floral dress she bought. She quickly rubbed it with her thumb. "I should be back tomorrow morning. I will call you when I land. Bye, mum, love you."

As she hung up the call, she sat for a moment to think about the argument she had with Obike last night and how he left her behind and went back to Nigeria. She wondered what would happen when she returned. First, she was certain that her father would swallow her passport and lock her up in her room forever, but before all that, there was one thing she had to do before she returned to Nigeria to submit to her fate.

As Nick grabbed his briefcase, he glanced around his apartment, hoping not to have forgotten anything before he embarked on his journey. Satisfied, he walked out of the room and slammed the door behind him. As he left his apartment, he stopped at the lobby to pick up the morning paper. Once in the back of the car, Nick's driver drove him to the airport.

After eating the breakfast that was served in her room, Stella quickly dressed up. She phoned the receptionist to call her a cab. Few minutes later, she grabbed her purse and left her room with the "do not disturb" tag facing front. As she walked through the narrow and beautifully decorated hallway, she wondered if she was doing the right thing. Her legs felt heavier with each step but she continued.

She needed to find out why Nick hadn't contacted her in a long time. If she didn't take this trip, she may never find out what happened to him; she may never have the opportunity to return to Canada. She had to summon courage to pay him a surprise visit. At least he could look her in the eyes and tell her that he didn't want her anymore before her wedding, which was in six days. She sat in the cab and told the driver where to take her to. Few minutes later, she arrived in front of the Walter's mansion and got out of the cab. As usual, Adolph walked up to her with a smile and ushered her in.

As she entered the living room, her eyes wandered around the heavily furnished room as if she hadn't been there before. The last time she visited was when Nick invited her for a family dinner, and of course she didn't forget how inquisitive Nick's father was with her throughout the whole evening. "Is Nick here?" she asked Adolph, who stood upright protectively. "He hasn't come in weeks, but Sir is upstairs getting ready for a meeting." She smiled and ran up the stairs, wondering which one was Mr. Walsh's room. She turned one last time and caught Adolph staring at her. He pointed at a big door by the corner of the hall. She smiled and drew a long breath as she gently tapped on the door.

Waiting for a response, she pressed her dress with her palms and observed her shoes as if she was attending an interview. "Adolph I need a hand with this button, come on in," she heard through the door. She gently

opened the door with her head in first. Seeing Mr.
Walsh struggling to button his cufflinks, she walked
closer to help him. "I thought it was Adolph. You
should be in Africa, right?" he asked with a stern look
on his face as his wrist hung loosely on Stella's hands.
"I came a week ago for a visit. Have you seen Nick?"
Now she was done with the buttons. She stepped
back and waited for him to respond.
"Did you think you can barge in here and ask me
after my son? He barely speaks to me ever since he
returned from that trip. I'm sure he has a cellphone.
Why don't you call him?"
"I did but it was switched off."
"Well he told me he would be traveling this week. He
didn't say where or the exact day."
"And you don't know when he will be back?"
"I just told you already."
"Sir, my father told me everything about your father."
At the mention of this Mr. Walsh quickly turned and
stared at Stella. He walked over to where his scotch
was hurdled in a table. He lifted a bottle of Bourbon
and poured the liquid into a glass.
"But that's not why I'm here." Stella continued.
"Then why are you here? As you can see, I don't have
your grandfather's diamonds, and Nick doesn't know
anything about it either, so what else do you want?"
he barked.
"I just want to see Nick. Can you tell him I dropped
by?"
"That won't be difficult, now would it?"
"Tell him to call me in five days. I shall return to
Nigeria tonight so I'll be expecting his call."
Mr. Walsh replied and gulped his drink. He picked

up his wrist watch and placed it on his wrist. He watched from the corner of his eyes as Stella turned to leave his room, but she stopped and turned to face him saying, "I really do love your son, sir. It's very important that you give him this message." With that, she exited the room.

As she sat back in the cab, she watched the houses disappear from her sight as the cab drove away. She wondered where Nick would go to and why his father hated her so much. At this point, it seemed the heavens were ready to wed her with or without Nick. At least she tried one last time, and it seemed like she was the only one who wanted this affair to work. Without any choice left, she went back to her hotel room and packed her things and left for the airport.

The next afternoon was followed by a heated argument with Chief Ndube and Obike's father, Chief Nwigwe. Upon Obike's return to Nigeria and narrating his ordeal with his wife to be, his father was very disappointed that he threatened to call off his investment in Chief Ndube's company as payback for not encouraging his daughter to get married to his son. Chief Ndube wasn't happy about this new development. Even though he knew what a good husband Obike would make for his daughter, having his father invest in his company was much more important to him.

"How do I explain this embarrassment to my friends and business partners flying from all over the world?" Obike's father roared as he wiped off a trickle of sweat traveling down his forehead.

"No one said the wedding has been canceled. They

are young and have probably developed cold feet, but that doesn't mean they don't want to get married," Chief Ndube replied, hoping that his friend wouldn't get worked up about the issue. He knew his stubborn daughter had caused it all, but all that was left was for her to confirm that the wedding still held or else he would lose it all.

"Then what prank was your daughter playing on my son in Canada? If she doesn't want to get married to him then I'll be sure to help him find a suitable girl."

"Ah, you are taking this matter so far, my friend. It hasn't gotten to that. Stella just arrived this morning and as soon I get home I will sort this out."

"You better. The wedding is in five days!"

"You have nothing to worry about. Tell your boy that the wedding still holds. Stella will surely call you to apologize, okay?" Chief Ndube assured him for the last time before he left the office and barked at his driver to take him home immediately.

Stella ran out to her bedroom as soon as she heard her phone ringing. She snatched the phone off the table and quickly answered. "Obi, where are you? We need to talk." She gasped from the little run she made from the bathroom to the bedroom. After the last visit to Nick's house, she felt that Nick wasn't coming back and all there was left was to make up with Obike and get married. "Obi, I am sorry. I know I was no good in Canada but we need to talk. Can we meet this afternoon?" She smiled when she was satisfied with his response, and quickly hung up the phone.

After a long wait, Obike arrived at her house with a stern look on his face. Mathew offered him a seat while he ran to inform Stella. As soon as she emerged from the hallway, Obike stood up and went to hug her. "No matter what happens between us, you will always remain my best friend," he said as he pecked her cheeks.

She didn't understand this kindness and love from him. She had hurt him many times and all he did was love her as many times as possible without grudges. As she sat down beside him, she gently took his hand and placed it on her cheeks with apologetic eyes.

"Where are we now?"

Obike looked at her and smiled, saying, "It doesn't matter anymore baby. It's okay if you don't want us. I am always here for you. I don't want this to ruin our friendship." Stella's eyes widened. She had expected him to snuggle her closer and tell her that he was still madly in love with her and beg her to marry him. She drew a long breath before asking the last question, which everyone wanted to hear; her father, her mother, Obike's father, Obike, and even herself.

"What about the wedding?"

Obike looked at her again and asked innocently, "What about it?"

"I thought you wanted to get married?"

"That was before you told me that you didn't want to get married," Obike replied and turned his face away. She stared at him for a couple of minutes, thinking of what to say next.

"Can we get by this and continue with the marriage plans?" Obike stared at her as the words escaped her mouth. Could she have meant what she just said or was it another joke to make him feel better, he wondered. "I've thought about the whole thing and I think getting married is not such a bad idea. I may have hung onto something that wasn't worth holding onto and now I think I want to be with you," she continued.

Obike didn't know whether to dance or hop in excitement, but as a man, he tried to keep his calm and simply asked, "Are you sure about this? Are you sure this is what you really want? Because I don't want to guilt you into anything that..." He was interrupted by a gentle kiss from Stella, which shut him up completely. He pulled her closer and kissed her deeper as she gasped for breath. She then pulled away from his grip and stared into his eyes and smiled. He smiled back and kissed her arm.

As Nick arrived in Lagos, he knew it would be a bad idea to go over to Stella's house after the last experience he had with her father. Chief Ndube had threatened to shoot him the next time he set foot in his house or anywhere around him, so there was no need turning that threat into reality. He decided to check into a hotel in Ajao Estate, closer to the airport. As he entered his room, he knew it was too late to visit or contact Stella. He knew he had to plan a romantic way to see her. As he undressed to shower, another thought invaded his mind; what if Stella didn't want to see him anymore? What if she declined his marriage proposal? How was he to even marry her without her parents' consent? He dashed to his luggage and rummaged through the side pocket and fished out a red ring box. He gently opened it to take another look at what he'd be presenting to Stella when he saw her. Satisfied, he smiled to himself and closed the box. This time he kept the box in a different side pocket where it would be easier for him to reach it next time.

As he finally stepped into the shower and let the towel loose, Obike crossed his mind. He remembered how friendly he was the first time they met in the mall in Canada, and how he had invited him to his wedding. If there were anyone worth seeking assistance from, it would be him. He would probably know where and how to meet Stella so he could easily propose to her, but first, he had to find his number and then give him a call. He knew how difficult his plans were going to be, but he was determined to pursue them. That would be after he had showered, rested, and was ready to hit the town.

Chapter 13

On the day before the wedding, the families gathered together to celebrate the couple. Chief Ndube couldn't express his joy enough; he kept dancing with his wife and daughter. The maids constantly appeared with trays filled with snacks and champagne. Stella was in the corner of the room with Chike's fiancée while Obike was chatting with his father. As the merriment continued, Obike received a call from an unknown number. He glanced at his phone, wondering whether to answer or reject it. He wondered who could be calling him by that hour, so he decided to return the call.

Upon recognizing that it was Nick, he grew excited. He didn't know that he would be in the country before the wedding, as promised. Overjoyed, Obike rushed outside, away from the noise of the party, to answer the call. After a short conversation on the phone, Obike promised to go and pay him a visit, or better still bring him over to meet his family. As soon as he ended the call, he turned around to find Stella standing at the door, staring at him. He was sure that she heard the entire conversation, so he smiled at her. With his eye glittering in the dark, he quickly shared his joy with her.

Stella wasn't as happy as he was but smiled weakly at him. She watched him dash into the house and whisper something to his father. After the party, Obike drove straight to the hotel where Nick was lodging. As soon as the men saw each other, they shook hands and went to chat at the lobby. "It's so good to see you mehn," Nick expressed as soon as he lowered himself on a plastic chair.

"Yeah mehn, I can't believe you made it. I told wifey and she was surprised too," Obike replied and waved at the waiter.

"Tomorrow is your big day, bro. You gotta do that walk, mehn," Nick teased him.

"I know! My heart is racing. I guess there's nothing wrong with having cold feet in this situation."

"I bet she's one lucky gal,"

"Oh you have no idea; she's the best thing that ever happened to me. I can't wait to make her mine forever. We've been friends since we were kids, and I guess this is God's will," Obike replied happily. He couldn't withhold his excitement from his newfound friend. "Why don't you join us tonight for my bachelor's party? The boys have arranged something for me tonight, so come chill with us since you are here all alone," Obike said.

Nick nodded as he spoke, thinking about his invitation, and finally gave in. "I'll go get changed then. Give me a few minutes." Obike ordered a bottle of water and sipped it as Nick went to his room to change. Few minutes later, the men left the hotel and Obike drove to a club downtown.

The next morning was a busy one as Stella's friends prepared her for the wedding. Martha came to the room to see her daughter well dressed up in her cream wedding dress with lace details around the hem. As the maids carried on with their duties, Chief Ndube and Professor Sunday dressed up in suits and chewed Kolanut that early morning.

"Oke enyi m—my dearest friend, the day that we've

all been anticipating and praying for has finally arrived. The auspicious moment is here," Prof. Sunday began. "How quick do children grow these days? I remember little Stella that used to play with my children, and now she's become a woman." Chief Ndube nodded agreeably as his friend spoke. He lifted a glass of champagne off the table and sipped it.

"Our people say that a child must learn to crawl first before walking." Professor Sunday nodded as Chief Ndube spoke. "We raised her well, and the time has come for her to prove it. I just wish our young girls will emulate this and set forth to marriage properly!"

As the friends discussed, Martha walked in with a huge smile on her face, saying to her husband, "Darling, your daughter is the most beautiful woman on earth today. Her dress fits perfectly."

Professor Sunday smiled and looked at his friend, who scuffed, "It is the pride of every father to watch his daughters get married. I have lived to that day and nothing will stop me from seeing her in that beautiful dress today."

Mathew, dressed in a rusty grey suit, quickly rushed in to announce that the car was ready. The men stood up and went into the waiting black SUV. Martha hurried back to Stella's room to announce the same. The women all walked gently into a waiting limousine, beaming a smile at one another. The cars rode off the compound and headed to the church. As Obike straightened the collar of his light lavender shirt, he suddenly remembered that he was supposed to send a driver to go and pick up Nick from the hotel. He quickly brought out his cellphone and ordered his driver to go and get him. He turned to his two friends who were getting ready as well and smiled, saying, "You all better get hooked tonight, cus I won't be hanging out with you guys no more if you are not planning to settle down." The men laughed out loud.

One of them replied, "How many of your female friends did you import from Chicago for this wedding?"

Obike shook his head and rolled a piece of paper and threw it at him. "I'm very serious guys. You better be catching something tonight, fellas," Obike repeated.

The second guy, who had kept quiet all through this, suddenly asked, "Is Stella's best friend gonna be there?"

Obike looked at him and asked, "Which of them?"

"The light skinned one from Canada?"

"I guess so. Stella told me she arrived in Lagos last night. Wait a minute, is that why you are coming to my wedding?" Obike asked his friend playfully.

The other men laughed. "C'mon, man, I think I like that babe. If she's what I think she is, you may be attending my wedding soon."

Obike, after recovering from a long fit of laughter, turned to his friend and said, "When I said you all need to hurry up, I didn't mean this bad boy here. He's always promising to get married each time he sees a woman. You know what? I won't even take you seriously until I see a wedding invitation."

The first man shook his head and slipped into his shoes, saying coyly, "Even after I see the wedding invitation, I still need to believe it after the wedding too, cus I don't trust this dude here." The men chatted and left for the church.

As Nick left his room and made his way towards the elevator, he knew it was about time to start making enquiries about Stella. He didn't discuss his quest with his friend because he didn't want to stress him before his wedding, so he thought it would be a good idea to wait until tonight. As he stopped before the large mirror at the reception, he parted his hair in a corner and adjusted his tie. Satisfied with his look, he matched towards the waiting car outside, which drove him to the church. As he stared at the large cathedral, his heart suddenly began racing. First, he hadn't been to a Nigerian wedding before, especially when he knew little about the groom, but he knew it would be fun to be surrounded with the tradition and, of course, learn how it's done, in case he decided to wed Stella. As the black limousine finally arrived with decorative balloons all around it, Nick thought to himself that it must be the bride. He hadn't gotten an opportunity to meet her, so he brought his head out of the car to catch a glimpse of her face, but the lady was much too focused and didn't look around as she walked gently with her friends into the church dressing room. Unhappy that he couldn't see the bride's face, he shrugged and stepped out of the car and headed to the church.

The church was filled with guests all dressed in different attires, and the choir humming a song. The priest prepared the altar as the church began cramming with guests. As Nick found a seat close to the altar, he glanced at his watch continuously as he tried to avoid the curious stares of other guests. Soon he heard noises outside and went to investigate the clamor. He saw Obike and his friends walking towards the dressing room in the church, with smiles on their faces.

Obike, seeing Nick at the entrance of the church, hugged him and they both went into the dressing room. Nick couldn't help but compliment his friend's dressing. As the men checked out their ties and shoes for the last time, satisfied, they all walked back into the church. By this time, only a few seats were left for guests. Nick sat down and waited for the ceremony to begin.

The priest quietly signaled the usher to alert Stella that it was time. Soon the tune of Johann Pachelbel's "Canon in D" filled the room as the little brides and grooms walked down the aisle, sprinkling lavender and white rose petals, followed by the bride's maids and groom's men holding hands as they walked up to the altar, beaming smiles at the guests.

Martha, who couldn't hold her happiness any longer, accompanied with the touching song, brought out a handkerchief from her purse and dabbed her eyes with it as she waited for her daughter to appear. The church quickly rose up as Chief Ndube led Stella, whose veil covered her beautiful face, down the aisle. As Nick stood up, he managed to catch a glimpse of Stella's eyes, but they didn't look his way. He felt a sudden rush as she walked past him. Speechless, he continued to stare as she went up to the altar, facing Obike. His heart began racing as he became anxious to see her face clearly.

"Who is giving this lady's hand in marriage today?" the priest asked as soon as the slow tune lowered.

"I, her father, am giving her off today," Chief Ndube replied with a big smile. He nodded at Obike and went to sit beside his wife. Obike lifted her veil, revealing those beautiful eyes for all to see, and most especially for Nick, who was frozen in his seat. Tears gathered around his eyes. The priest shared a few sermons from the Bible and went on to join the duo. "Do you have the ring?" the priest asked. Obike turned to his best man for the ring, but as the man dipped his hand into his pocket, the ring was nowhere to be found. The church murmured as the man began searching for the ring. He whispered into Obike's ears as he frowned and whispered to the priest. One of Obike's friends, who recognized what was happening, squeezed out of his fancy male golden ring and gave it to Obike, but the female ring was nowhere in place.

Nick stood up and walked to the altar. As Stella saw his face, she felt chills all over. She wanted to scream and hug him, but she was at the last road to do so. Nick dipped his hand into his pocket and brought out the engagement ring he had bought for her and handed it to Obike with a smile. Stella couldn't take her eyes off him. Nick turned around and walked out of the church. No one knew what was happening but the ceremony continued.

Stella felt she could absorb through everything as she tried to regain her composure. She couldn't hear what the priest was saying and when she lifted her eyes to look at Obike, he smiled at her and couldn't catch the worry in her face. She turned around and bolted from the church in pursuit of Nick with her dress floating in the air. The church was in a commotion as Chief

Ndube rose up and bit his lips angrily. Obike rubbed his head as if he knew something like this could happen.

As Stella chased down Nick who was about to enter the car he came with, she quickly grabbed his hand and hugged him as tears rolled down her cheeks. He was surprised to see her and brought out a handkerchief from his pocket and dabbed off the tears, which were already messing up her makeup.

"Nick, what is this? What are you doing here?" Stella managed to ask as she choked in her tears.

"I didn't know you were getting married. Your husband invited me when he came to Canada. I planned to come and meet you and…"

"And propose to me?" Stella interrupted. "How dare you? I went to your house but your father told me you traveled!"

"I was coming to you, baby."

"No phone calls, no emails."

"I'm sorry, baby. I did call but your number wasn't going through either. Your dad threatened to kill me if I ever came close to you," Nick explained again as he held her close.

"The roses, did you send them?"

"Yes, I did."

"And now what is our fate?" Stella asked.

"I'm sorry, baby, but I have to go now. Please stop crying...don't do this. That man loves you very much."

"More than you do?" Stella queried tearfully

"I've always loved you Stella, and I will forever, but he loves you too."

"You show your face here with an engagement

ring and you dare tell me to go and marry someone else?" Stella screamed in anger.

"This will kill him. Obike loves you," Nick preached as he withheld his own tears. "It will never work out for the two of us. Your family despises me."

"We can run away. Far away from their hate, Nick, we can."

"I know, but that won't be right. I am sorry, baby. We have to let this go."

"No, Nick, I won't, I can't. You live in me!" she cried and beat her chest.

"I'm sorry, baby."

"No, Nick, you won't leave me this time. I won't let that happen," she wheezed.

As the couple argued, they failed to notice Obike and Chief Ndube standing behind them with a confused look on their faces. "What is going on here?" Chief Ndube barked.

"I have to go Stella, I wish you a happy married life, sweetie. I will send some gifts when I get to Canada," Nick said as he avoided looking at her father.

Stella shook her head vehemently as more tears poured. She turned to her father crying and saying, "Dad are you gonna let him go for the second time, are you?"

Chief Ndube for the first time felt emotional as he stared at the young lovers crying. He hadn't seen his daughter cry so much for something. This made him realize how much she loved Nick.

Obike went straight to Stella and asked, "Is he the man you told me about?" Stella nodded and stared at him with her eyes pleading for forgiveness. "And you love him?" Stella nodded as well.

Obike turned to Chief Ndube and said, "Sir, of what use will it be to be married to a woman who may never love you like she loves another? A woman who will imagine another holding her when she's with you? What use will it be to force her to marry me knowing that she will never be happy?" Chief Ndube sighed. "I love your daughter first as a best friend and then as a partner, and I hate to see her cry or deny her happiness." Chief Ndube shook his head at Obike, a young man speaking from pain and love. "I may never find another best friend, but I can still find love someday. "

Stella went to Obike and knelt in front of him, crying, "Obi, I am sorry, please forgive me."

Obike helped her up and patted the strands of hair covering her face and said, "It doesn't matter anymore. You've chosen who you want to be with. Now go and get married before you lose him again." Chief Ndube was speechless as he wiped off sweat from his neck. On a second glare at Nick, he exhaled anger from his nostrils as he approached him. "I thought I warned you never to come close to my family again?"

Nick drew a long breath and dragged Stella by the hand towards her father, saying, "Is this what you want for your daughter? Look at her, she's unhappy and you don't even care for her tears?"

"You are not in the position to make her happy either," Chief Ndube retorted.

"Yes I can go forever and never come back, but what exactly did I do to you? I don't even know the foundation of this hatred, but am I to suffer for what my grandfather did?"

"Yelling at me is not an option boy! Your family ruined my family!"

"And I've come to make things right! Allow me into your family, sir, for the sake of your daughter!" Chief Ndube was now embarrassed as the crowd stared at him as if he was hardhearted and interrupting the wedding. He then walked away from the crowd and headed back to the church as he thought about the argument with Nick. As he stood at the church entrance, he turned around and called out to Nick and Stella, "What are you two still standing there for? Hurry before I change my mind forever!" Stella glanced at Nick and smiled. They both went back into the church, and this time the song was played again, but with Nick as the groom.

As Stella emerged from the dressing room, her father took her hand and Obike took the other, standing at her left. As they both walked her down the aisle, she continued to stare at Obike's plain face. Filled with guilt, she squeezed his hand and whispered a thank you as they walked. She thought in her mind and searched his face as they walked,

You don't speak, you don't even ask for a lot
Whatever you give, you give with your heart
You have enough love for the both of us
You don't even care about receiving but give out with a
smile
You are hiding your grief to make me happy
You are light, you are beautiful inside and out and you are
mine
You are the best friend I can ever think of
I know I owe you all but wish I could give you all.

As they approached the altar, the priest repeated his question again, "Who is giving this lady's hand for marriage?" Obike and Chief Ndube looked at each other and smiled saying, "We are." After a short sermon from the bible and exchange of vows, they were pronounced man and wife. They ran off the church like teenagers and the waiting limousine drove them home. After the wedding reception that took place that evening, Stella and Nick left for Canada few days later to plan their lives.

Obike returned to Chicago to practice medicine and got married two years after to his MD's daughter. Nick's father died a year later and Nick invested in Chief Ndube's company and built a bigger diamond company in Abuja, Nigeria and made Chike, Stella's elder brother, his manager while he stayed in Canada with his wife. The family ties became inseparable.

The End.

MORE FROM THIS AUTHOR

Burning Wind ©2012

Synopsis - After the loss of her parents and her innocence, everything about Brenda came to a halt; her life, her emotions, her ability to see herself as a young woman. In this heart touching story, forgiveness will be farfetched as Brenda's anger pushes her to an irreversible extent.

Treasure of Mine